Praise for PATRICK MODIANO *and*

So You Don't Get Lost in the Neighborhood

"Modiano is an ideal writer to gorge on . . . in part because [his books] make up a system as beguiling and complete as any in contemporary literature . . . In [*So You Don't Get Lost in the Neighborhood*], Modiano has set up a moody, delectable noir."
— *The New Yorker*

"[Modiano's] fiction resonates so deeply [because] it occupies an elusive middle ground between place and personality . . . Compelling."
— *Los Angeles Times*

"A suspenseful inquiry into memory and storytelling, including the stories we tell ourselves about our own lives. It's the best kind of mystery, the kind that never stops haunting you. **A–**."
— *Entertainment Weekly*

"A writer unlike any other and a worthy recipient of the Nobel."
— *Wall Street Journal*

"Modiano combines a detective's curiosity with an elegist's melancholy."
— *New Republic*

"An author with a virtuoso's command of language, equally at ease with the simple and the complex, the precise and the evocative."
— *New York Review of Books*

"Euan Cameron's atmospheric translation does ample justice to this spectral tale."
— *Independent*

"The more Modiano you read, the more seductive his work becomes . . . Hypnotic and compulsive."
— *Telegraph*

So You Don't Get Lost in the Neighborhood

Works by Patrick Modiano in English translation

The Occupation Trilogy
(La Place de l'Étoile, The Night Watch, Ring Roads)

Lacombe, Lucien (with Louis Malle)

Missing Person

Honeymoon

Out of the Dark

Dora Bruder

Catherine Certitude

Suspended Sentences: Three Novellas

Pedigree: A Memoir

So You Don't Get Lost in the Neighborhood

After the Circus

Paris Nocturne

PATRICK MODIANO

So You Don't Get Lost in the Neighborhood

A Novel

Translated from the French by Euan Cameron

Mariner Books
Houghton Mifflin Harcourt
Boston   New York

First Mariner Books edition 2016

First U.S. edition

Copyright © 2014 by Editions Gallimard, Paris

English translation copyright © 2015 by Euan Cameron

First published in France as *Pour que tu ne te perdes pas dans le quartier*
by Editions Gallimard, Paris, 2014.

This translation first published in the United Kingdom
by MacLehose Press, an imprint of Quercus, in 2015.

Library of Congress Cataloging-in-Publication Data
Modiano, Patrick, 1945–
[Pour que tu ne te perdes pas dans le quartier. English]
So you don't get lost in the neighborhood / Patrick Modiano ;
translated by Euan Cameron.
pages cm
"First published in France as Pour que tu ne te perdes pas dans le quartier
by Editions Gallimard, Paris, 2014" — Verso title page.
ISBN 978-0-544-63506-7 (hardback) — ISBN 978-0-544-63507-4 (ebook) —
ISBN 978-0-544-81186-7 (pbk.)
1. Psychological fiction. I. Cameron, Euan (translator) translator. II. Title.
PQ2673.O3P6813 2015
843'.914 — dc23
2015017303

Printed in the United States of America
DOC 10 9 8 7 6 5 4 3 2 1

I cannot provide the reality of events,
I can only convey their *shadow*.

STENDHAL

ALMOST NOTHING. LIKE AN INSECT BITE THAT INITIALLY strikes you as very slight. At least that is what you tell yourself in a low voice so as to reassure yourself. The telephone had rung at about four o'clock in the afternoon at Jean Daragane's home, in the room that he called the "study". He was dozing on the sofa at the far end, shielded from the sunlight. And these ringing sounds, which he had been unaccustomed to hearing for a long time, went on continuously. Why this insistence? Perhaps they had forgotten to ring off at the other end of the line. Finally, he got to his feet and walked over to the area of the room near the windows, where the sun was beating down too strongly.

"I should like to speak to Monsieur Jean Daragane."

A dreary and threatening voice. That was his first impression.

"Monsieur Daragane? Can you hear me?"

Daragane wanted to hang up. But what was the point? The ringing would start again, without ever stopping. And, short of cutting the telephone cord permanently . . .

"This is he."

"It's about your address book, monsieur."

He had lost it last month on a train that was taking him to the Côte d'Azur. Yes, it could only have been in this train. The address book had probably slipped from his coat pocket just as he was taking out his ticket to hand it to the collector.

"I found an address book with your name on it."

Written on the grey cover was: IF FOUND RETURN THIS NOTEBOOK TO. And one day, without thinking, Daragane had jotted down his name there, his address and his telephone number.

"I'll bring it to your home. On whatever day and time would suit you."

Yes, a dreary and threatening voice, for sure. And even, Daragane thought, the tone of a blackmailer.

"I'd prefer us to meet somewhere else."

He had made an effort to overcome his uneasiness. But his voice, which he intended to sound detached, suddenly struck him as flat.

"As you wish, monsieur."

There was a silence.

"That's a shame. I'm very close to where you live. I should have liked to hand it over to you personally."

Daragane wondered whether the man was not standing outside the building and whether he would remain there, waiting for him to come out. He had to be got rid of as quickly as possible.

"Let's see each other tomorrow afternoon," he said eventually.

"If you like. But it will have to be close to where I work. Near the gare Saint-Lazare."

He was on the point of hanging up, but he kept his composure.

"Do you know rue de l'Arcade?" the other man asked. "We could meet at a café. At 42 rue de l'Arcade."

Daragane jotted down the address. He recovered his breath and said:

'Very well, monsieur. At 42 rue de l'Arcade, tomorrow, at five in the afternoon."

Then he rang off without waiting for the other person to reply. He immediately regretted behaving in such an abrupt way, but he put it down to the heat that had been hanging over Paris for several days, a heat that was unusual for September. It emphasised his loneliness. It forced him to remain shut up in this room until sunset. And then the telephone had not rung for months. As for the mobile, on his desk, he wondered when he had last used it. He scarcely knew how it operated and frequently made mistakes when he pressed the buttons.

If the stranger had not phoned, he would have totally forgotten the loss of this address book. He tried to recall the names that were in it. The week before, he had even wanted to start a new one and had begun to compose a list on a sheet of white paper. After a short while, he had torn it up. None of the names belonged to people who had mattered in his life: he had never needed to write down their addresses and phone numbers. He knew them by heart. In this note-book there were nothing but contacts of a so-called "profes-sional nature", a few supposedly useful addresses, no more than about thirty names. And among them several that should have been deleted, because they were no longer current. The only thing that had bothered him about the loss of this notebook was that he had written his own name in it, as well as his address. He could, of course, not keep his promise and leave this person waiting vainly at 42 rue de l'Arcade. But then there would always be something unresolved, a threat. At a low ebb on certain solitary afternoons, he had often dreamt that the telephone would ring and that a gentle voice would make a date with him. He remembered the title of a novel he had read: *Le Temps des rencontres*. Perhaps that time of meetings was not yet over for him. But the voice he had just heard did not fill him with confidence. Both dreary and threatening, that voice. Yes.

He asked the taxi driver to drop him at the Madeleine. It was not as hot as on other days and it was possible to walk as long as one chose the pavement that was in the shade. He followed the rue de l'Arcade, deserted and silent in the sunshine.

He had not been in this vicinity for ages. He remembered that his mother once acted in a nearby theatre and that his father had an office at the very end of the street, on the left, at 73 boulevard Haussmann. He was astonished that he still remembered the number 73. But all this past had become so translucent with time . . . a mist that dissipated in the sunlight.

The café was on the corner of the street that adjoined boulevard Haussmann. An empty room, a long counter with shelves built above it, as in a self-service store or a former Wimpy. Daragane sat down at one of the tables at the back. Would this stranger turn up for the appointment? Both doors were open, the one that gave onto the street and the one onto the boulevard, because of the heat. On the other side of the road stood the large building at 73 . . . He wondered whether one of the windows of his father's office had not overlooked that side of the street. Which floor? But these memories drifted away like bubbles of soap or fragments of a dream that vanished on waking. His memory would have been livelier in the café in rue des Mathurins, opposite the theatre, where he used to wait for his mother, or in the close vicinity of the gare Saint-Lazare, an area he had known well in the past. But no. It would not have been. It was no longer the same city.

"Monsieur Jean Daragane?"

He had recognised the voice. A man of about forty was standing in front of him, accompanied by a girl younger than him.

"Gilles Ottolini."

It was the same voice, dreary and threatening. He gestured towards the girl:

"A friend . . . Chantal Grippay."

Daragane remained seated on the bench, not moving, and not even offering to shake hands with them. They both sat down opposite him.

"Please forgive us . . . We're a little late."

He had adopted a tongue-in-cheek tone, so as to put on a good front no doubt. Yes, it was the same voice with a slight, almost imperceptible, Southern accent that Daragane had not noticed on the telephone the previous evening.

An ivory-coloured skin, dark eyes, an aquiline nose. The face was slender, as angular at the front as it was in profile.

"Here's your property," he said to Daragane, in the same tongue-in-cheek tone that seemed to conceal a certain embarrassment.

And he took out the address book from his coat pocket. He placed it on the table, covering it with his hand, his fingers splayed. It was as though he wanted to prevent Daragane from picking it up.

The girl sat back slightly, as though she did not want to draw attention to herself, a brunette of about thirty years old, with mid-length hair. She was wearing a black blouse and black trousers. She glanced anxiously at Daragane. Because of her cheekbones and her slanting eyes, he wondered whether she was not of Vietnamese extraction originally – or Chinese.

"And where did you find this notebook?"

"On the floor, underneath a bench in the cafeteria at the gare de Lyon."

He handed him the address book. Daragane thrust it into his pocket. He remembered, in fact, that on the day of his departure for the Côte d'Azur he had arrived early at the gare de Lyon and that he had sat down in the cafeteria on the first floor.

"Would you like something to drink?" asked the man called Gilles Ottolini.

Daragane wanted to be rid of them. But he changed his mind.

"A tonic water."

"Try to catch someone to take the order. I'll have a coffee," said Ottolini, turning towards the girl.

She stood up immediately. Clearly, she was used to obeying him.

"It must have been annoying for you to have lost this notebook..."

He gave an odd sort of smile which struck Daragane as insolent. But perhaps it was awkwardness on his part or shyness.

"You know," said Daragane, "I hardly use the telephone anymore."

The other man looked at him in astonishment. The girl came back to their table and sat down again.

"They're no longer serving at this hour. They're about to close."

It was the first time Daragane heard this girl's voice, a voice that was husky and that did not have the slight Southern accent of the man sitting next to her. Rather more of a Parisian one, if that still means anything.

"Do you work in the area?" asked Daragane.

"In an advertising agency in rue Pasquier. The Sweerts agency."

"And you too?"

He had turned towards the girl.

"No," said Ottolini, without allowing the girl time to reply. "She doesn't do anything at the moment." And once again that contorted smile. The girl also gave a flicker of a smile.

Daragane was in a hurry to get away. If he did not do so straight away, would he manage to get rid of them?

"I'll be frank with you . . ." He was leaning towards Daragane, and his voice was shriller.

Daragane experienced the same feeling as he had the previous day, on the telephone. Yes, this man had the persistence of an insect.

"I took the liberty of leafing through your address book . . . simple curiosity . . ."

The girl had looked away, as if pretending not to hear.

"You're not angry with me?"

Daragane looked him straight in the eyes. The other man held his gaze.

"Why should I be angry?"

A silence. The man had eventually lowered his gaze. Then, in the same metallic voice:

"There's someone whose name I found in your address book. I should like you to give me some information about him . . ."

His tone of voice had become more humble.

"Forgive my inquisitiveness . . ."

"Whom does it concern?" asked Daragane reluctantly.

He suddenly felt the need to get to his feet and to step out quickly through the open door onto boulevard Haussmann. And to breathe in the fresh air.

"A certain Guy Torstel."

He stressed each syllable of the surname and the first name carefully, as if to awaken the other's dormant memory.

"Who did you say?"

"Guy Torstel."

Daragane took the address book from his pocket and opened it at the letter T. He read the name, at the very top of the page, but this Guy Torstel meant nothing to him.

"I can't imagine who this could be."

"Really?"

The man seemed disappointed.

"There's a seven-digit phone number," said Daragane. "It must date back at least thirty years . . ."

He turned over the pages. All the other phone numbers were current ones. With ten digits. And he had only been using this address book for five years.

"This name means nothing to you?"

"No."

A few years earlier, he would have displayed some of that

politeness for which he was renowned. He would have said: "Give me a bit of time to throw some light on the mystery . . ." But the words did not come.

"It's to do with a news item about which I've gathered quite a lot of information," the man continued. "This name is mentioned. That's all . . ."

He suddenly seemed to be on the defensive.

"What kind of news item?"

Daragane has asked the question automatically, as though he were rediscovering his former courteous reflexes.

"A very old news item . . . I wanted to write an article about it . . . You know, I used to do some journalism to begin with . . ."

But Daragane's attention was flagging. He really must get rid of them quickly, otherwise this man was going to tell him his life story.

"I'm sorry," he told him. "I've forgotten this Torstel . . . At my age, one suffers memory losses . . . I must leave you unfortunately . . ."

He stood up and shook hands with both of them. Ottolini gave him a hard stare, as though Daragane had insulted him and he was ready to respond in a violent way. The girl, for her part, had lowered her gaze.

He walked over towards the wide-open glass door that gave

onto boulevard Haussmann, hoping that the man would not block his path. Outside, he breathed in deeply. What a strange idea, this meeting with a stranger, when he himself had not seen anybody for three months and was none the worse for it . . . On the contrary. In his solitude, he had never felt so light-hearted, with strange moments of elation either in the morning or the evening, as though everything were still possible and, as the title of the old film has it, adventure lay at the corner of the street . . . Never, even during the summers of his youth, had life seemed so free of oppression as it had since the beginning of this summer. But in summer, everything is uncertain – a "metaphysical" season, his philosophy teacher, Maurice Caveing, had once told him. It was odd, he remembered the name "Caveing" yet he no longer knew who this Torstel was.

It was still sunny, and a light breeze was cooling the heat. Boulevard Haussmann was deserted at this time of day.

Over the course of the past fifty years, he had often come here, and had done so even during his childhood, when his mother took him to Printemps, the large department store a little further up the boulevard. But this evening, his city seemed unfamiliar to him. He had cast off all the bonds that could still bind him to her, but perhaps it was she who had rejected him.

He sat down on a bench and took out the address book from his pocket. He was about to tear it up and scatter the shreds into the green plastic wastepaper bin beside the bench. Yet he hesitated. No, he would do so later, at home, when he had peace of mind. He leafed through the notebook absent-mindedly. Among these telephone numbers, there was not one that he would have wanted to dial. And then, the two or three missing numbers, those that had mattered to him and which he still knew by heart, would no longer respond.

AT ABOUT NINE O'CLOCK IN THE MORNING, THE telephone rang. He had just woken up.

"Monsieur Daragane? Gilles Ottolini."

The voice sounded less aggressive than the previous day.

"I'm sorry about yesterday . . . I feel that I annoyed you . . ."

The tone was courteous, and even deferential. None of that insect-like insistence that had so irritated Daragane.

"Yesterday . . . I wanted to catch up with you in the street . . . You left so abruptly . . ."

A silence. But this one was not threatening.

"You know, I've read a few of your books. *Le Noir de l'été* in particular . . ."

Le Noir de l'été. It took him a few seconds to realise that this was actually a novel that he had once written. His first book. It was so long ago . . .

"I liked *Le Noir de l'été* very much. This name that is

mentioned in your address book and that we spoke about . . .
Torstel . . . you used it in *Le Noir de l'été*."

Daragane had no memory of it. Nor of the rest of the book, for that matter.

"Are you sure?"

"You simply mention this name . . ."

"I must reread *Le Noir de l'eté*. But I haven't a single copy of it left."

"I could lend you mine."

The tone of voice struck Daragane as more terse, almost insolent. He was probably mistaken. When you have been too long on your own – he had not spoken to anyone since the beginning of the summer – you become suspicious and touchy towards your fellow men and you risk assessing them incorrectly. No, they are not as bad as all that.

"We didn't have time to go into any detail yesterday . . . But what is it you want to know about this Torstel . . .?"

Daragane had rediscovered his cheerful voice. It was just a matter of talking to someone. It was a bit like gymnastic exercises that restore your suppleness.

"Apparently he was involved in some old news item . . . The next time we see each other, I'll show you all the documents . . . I told you that I was writing an article about it . . ."

So this individual wished to see him again. Why not? For

some time he had felt some reluctance at the notion that newcomers might enter into his life. But, at other times, he still felt receptive. It depended on the day. Eventually, he said to him:

"So, what can I do for you?"

"I have to be away for two days because of my work. I'll phone you when I'm back. And we can arrange to meet."

"If you like."

He was no longer in the same mood as he was yesterday. He had probably been unfair with this Gilles Ottolini and had seen him in an unfavourable light. This was to do with the telephone ringing the other afternoon, which had roused him suddenly from his semi-slumber . . . A ringing sound heard so rarely in the past few months that it had given him a fright and had seemed to him just as threatening as if someone had come and knocked on his door at daybreak.

He did not want to reread *Le Noir de l'été*, even though reading it would give him the impression that the novel had been written by someone else. He would quite simply ask Gilles Ottolini to photocopy the pages that referred to Torstel. Would that be enough to remind him of anything?

He opened his notebook at the letter *T*, underlined "Guy Torstel 423 40 55" in blue ballpoint pen and added a question mark alongside the name. He had recopied all these pages from an old address book, crossing out the names of those who had died and the out-of-date numbers. And this Guy Torstel had probably slipped to the very top of the page because of a momentary lack of concentration on his part. He would have to find the old address book, which must date from about thirty years ago, and perhaps he would be reminded of him once he saw this name alongside other names from the past.

But today he did not have the courage to rummage around in cupboards and drawers. Still less to reread *Le Noir de l'été*. Besides, for some time his reading had been reduced to just one author: Buffon. He derived a great deal of comfort from him, thanks to the clarity of his style, and he regretted not having been influenced by him: writing novels whose characters might have been animals, and even trees or flowers ... If anyone were to have asked him nowadays which writer he might have wished to have been, he would have replied without hesitation: a Buffon of trees and flowers.

THE TELEPHONE RANG IN THE AFTERNOON, AT THE same time as the other day, and he thought that it was Gilles Ottolini once again. But no, a female voice.

"Chantal Grippay. Do you remember? We saw each other yesterday with Gilles . . . I don't want to disturb you . . ."

The voice was faint, muffled by interference.

A silence.

"I should very much like to see you, Monsieur Daragane. To talk to you about Gilles . . ."

The voice was clearer now. Evidently, this Chantal Grippay had overcome her shyness.

"Yesterday evening after you left, he was worried that you might be angry with him. He's spending two days in Lyon for his work . . . Could we see one another in the late afternoon?"

The tone of voice of this Chantal Grippay had become

more confident, like a diver who has paused for a few moments before jumping into the water.

"Some time around five o'clock, would that suit you? I live at 118 rue de Charonne."

Daragane jotted down the address on the same page that contained the name Guy Torstel.

"On the fourth floor, at the end of the corridor. The name's written on the letter box down below. It says Joséphine Grippay, but I've changed my first name . . ."

"At 118 rue de Charonne. At six in the evening . . . fourth floor," Daragane repeated.

"Yes, that's right . . . We'll talk about Gilles . . ."

After she had hung up, the phrase she had just uttered, "We'll talk about Gilles", echoed in Daragane's head like the ending of an alexandrine. He must ask her why she had changed her first name.

A brick building, taller than the others and slightly set back. Daragane preferred to climb the four storeys on foot rather than take the lift. At the end of the corridor, on the door, a visiting card in the name of "Joséphine Grippay". The first name "Joséphine" was scratched out and replaced, in violet ink, by "Chantal". He was on the point of ringing, but the door opened. She was wearing black, as at the café the other day.

"The bell doesn't work anymore, but I heard the sound of your footsteps."

She was smiling and she remained standing there, in the doorway. It was as though she were unsure whether to let him enter.

"We can go and have a drink somewhere else, if you like," said Daragane.

"Not at all. Come in."

A medium-sized room and, on the right, an open door. It apparently led to the bathroom. A light bulb was hanging from the ceiling.

"There's not much room here. But it's easier for us to talk."

She walked over to the small pale wooden desk between the two windows, drew out the chair and placed it by the bed.

"Do sit down."

She herself sat on the edge of the bed, or rather of the mattress, for the bed did not have a base.

"It's my room . . . Gilles found something larger for himself in the 17th, square du Graisivaudan."

She looked up to speak to him. He would have preferred to sit on the floor, or next to her, on the edge of the bed.

"Gilles is counting on you a great deal to help him write this article . . . He's written a book, you know, but he didn't dare tell you . . ."

And she leant back on the bed, reached out her arm and picked up a book with a green cover on the bedside table.

"Here . . . Don't tell Gilles that I lent it to you . . ."

A slim volume entitled *Le Flâneur hippique*, the back cover of which indicated that it had been published three years earlier by Sablier. Daragane opened it and glanced at the contents list. The book consisted of two main chapters: "Racecourses" and "School for Jockeys".

She gazed at him with her slightly slanting eyes.

"It's best that he doesn't know we've seen one another."

She stood up, went to close one of the windows that was half-open and sat down again on the edge of the bed. Daragane had the impression that she had closed this window so that they should not be heard.

"Before working for Sweerts, Gilles wrote articles on racecourses and horses for magazines and specialist papers."

She paused like someone who is about to let you into a secret.

"When he was very young, he went to the school for jockeys at Maisons-Laffitte. But it was too tough . . . he had to give it up . . . You'll see, if you read the book . . ."

Daragane listened to her carefully. It was strange to enter into people's lives so quickly . . . He had thought that this would be unlikely to happen to him any longer at his age, through weariness on his part and because of the feeling that other people slowly grow away from you.

"He used to take me to race meetings . . . He taught me to gamble . . . It's a drug, you know . . ."

All of a sudden, she seemed sad. Daragane wondered whether she might be seeking some sort of support from him, material or moral. And the solemnity of these words that had just crossed his mind made him want to laugh.

"And do you still go and place bets at race meetings?"

"Less and less since he's been working at Sweerts."

Her voice had dropped. Perhaps she feared that Gilles Ottolini might walk into the room unexpectedly and catch them both by surprise.

"I'll show you the notes that he put together for his article . . . Perhaps you've known all these people . . ."

"What people?"

"For instance, the person whom he spoke to you about . . . Guy Torstel . . ."

Once again, she leant back on the bed and took from beneath the bedside table a sky-blue cardboard folder which she opened. It contained typewritten pages and a book which she handed to him: *Le Noir de l'été*.

"I'd prefer you to keep it," he said brusquely.

"He marked the page where you mention this Guy Torstel . . ."

"I'll ask him to photocopy it. That will save me from having to reread the book . . ."

She seemed astonished that he should not want to reread his book.

"In a moment, we'll also go and make a photocopy of the notes he made so that you can take them with you."

And she pointed to the typewritten notes.

"But all this must remain between ourselves . . ."

Daragane was feeling slightly uncomfortable sitting on his chair and, so as to appear more composed, he leafed through Gilles Ottolini's book. In the chapter on "Racecourses", he came across two words printed in capital letters: LE TREMBLAY. And these words triggered something in him, without him quite knowing why, as though he was gradually being reminded of a detail that he had forgotten.

"You'll see . . . It's an interesting book . . ."

She looked up at him and smiled.

"Have you lived here long?"

"Two years."

The beige walls that had certainly not been repainted for years, the small desk, and the two windows that overlooked a courtyard . . . He had lived in identical rooms, at the age of this Chantal Grippay, and when he was younger than her. But at the time it was not in the eastern districts of the city.

Rather more to the south, on the outskirts of the 14th or the 15th arrondissement. And towards the north-east, square du Graisivaudan, which by a mysterious coincidence she had mentioned earlier. And also, at the foot of the butte Montmartre, between Pigalle and Blanche.

"I know that Gilles called you this morning before setting off for Lyon. Did he say anything in particular?"

"Just that we would be seeing one another again."

"He was frightened that you might be angry . . ."

Perhaps Gilles Ottolini was aware of their meeting today. He was reckoning that she would be more persuasive than he at encouraging him to talk, like those police inspectors who take over from one another during an interrogation. No, he had not left for Lyon and he was listening to their conversation behind the door. This thought made him smile.

"I'm being inquisitive, but I wonder why you've changed your first name."

"I reckoned that Chantal was simpler than Joséphine."

She had said this seriously, as if this change of names had been carefully considered.

"I have the impression that there are no Chantals at all nowadays. How did you come across this name?"

"I chose it from the almanac."

She had placed the sky-blue folder on the bed, beside her.

A large photograph was half protruding from it, in between the copy of *Le Noir de l'été* and the typewritten pages.

"What's this photograph?"

"A photo of a child . . . you'll see . . . It belonged in the dossier . . ."

He did not care for this word "dossier".

"Gilles was able to get some information from the police about the news item that interests him . . . We knew a cop who used to bet on horses . . . He searched around in the archives . . . He came across the photo as well . . ."

Once again she was speaking in that same husky voice, surprising in someone of her age, that she had used the other day in the café.

"Do you mind?" asked Daragane. "I'm too high up in this chair."

He came and sat on the floor, at the foot of the bed. Now they were on the same level.

"Not at all . . . you're uncomfortable there . . . Come onto the bed . . ."

She leant over to him, and her face was so close to his that he noticed a tiny scar on her left cheek. Le Tremblay. Chantal. Square du Graisivaudan. These words had travelled a long way. An insect bite, very slight to begin with, and it causes you an increasingly sharp pain, and very soon a feeling of being torn apart. The present and the past merge together, and that seems quite natural because they were only separated by a cellophane partition. An insect bite was all it took to pierce the cellophane. He could not be sure of the year, but he was very young, in a room as small as this one with a girl called Chantal – a fairly common name at the time. The husband of this Chantal, one Paul, and other friends of theirs had set off as they always did on Saturdays to gamble in the casinos on the outskirts of Paris: Enghien, Forges-les-Eaux . . . and they came back the following day with a bit of money. He, Daragane, and this Chantal, spent the entire night together in this room in square du Graisivaudan until the others returned. Paul, the husband, also used to go to race meetings. A gambler. With him it was not merely a matter of doubling up on your losses.

The other Chantal – the present-day one – stood up and opened one of the two windows. It was beginning to get very hot in this room.

"I'm waiting for a phone call from Gilles. I'm not going to tell him you're here. You promise me that you're going to help him?"

Once again he had the feeling that they had agreed, she and Gilles Ottolini, not to allow him any breathing space and to make appointments with him each in turn. But to what purpose? And to help in what way, precisely? To write his article on this old news item about which he, Daragane, still knew nothing? Perhaps the "dossier" – as she had said a moment ago – that file, there, beside her on the bed in its open cardboard folder, would provide him with some explanations.

"You promise me you'll help him?"

She was more persistent and was shaking her index finger. He was not sure whether this gesture was a threat.

"On condition that he informs me exactly what it is he wants from me."

A loud ringing sound came from the bathroom. Then, a few notes of music.

"My mobile . . . That must be Gilles . . ."

She went into the bathroom and closed the door behind her, as though she did not want Daragane to hear her talking. He sat down on the edge of the bed. He had not noticed a hat stand, on the wall by the entrance, from which hung a dress that looked to him as though it was made of black satin. A gold lamé swallow had been sewn on either side, beneath the shoulders. Zips shone from the hip and at the wrists. An old dress, probably picked up at the flea market. He imagined her in this black satin dress, with the two yellow swallows.

Behind the bathroom door, long periods of silence and,

each time, Daragane thought the conversation was over. But he heard her say in her husky voice: "No, I promise you . . ." and this phrase was repeated two or three times. He also heard her say "No, it's not true" and "It's much simpler than you think . . ." Apparently, Gilles Ottolini was blaming her for something or telling her about his anxieties. And she wanted to reassure him.

The conversation went on, and Daragane was tempted to leave the room without making any noise. When he was younger, he used the slightest opportunity to slip away from people, without his being able to understand very clearly why he did so: a longing to break free and to breathe in the fresh air? But today, he felt the need to let himself go with the tide, without pointless resistance. From out of the sky-blue cardboard folder he took the photograph that had caught his attention a moment ago. At first sight, it looked as though it was an enlargement of a passport photograph. A boy of about seven years old, with short hair cut in the style of the early fifties, though it could also be a present-day boy. One lived in a period when all the fashions, those of the past, yesterday and today, merged together, and perhaps, for children, it was a return to this earlier style of cutting. He would have to clear this up and he was keen to examine the way children's hair was cut, out there on the streets.

She emerged from the bathroom, her mobile in her hand.

"Forgive me . . . That went on a long time, but I put him in a much better mood. Sometimes, Gilles sees the gloomy side of everything."

She sat down next to him, on the side of the bed.

"That's why you have to help him. He would be so pleased if you could remember who this Torstel was . . . You don't have any idea?"

Yet more questioning. How late into the night would this go on? He would never get out of this room. Perhaps she had locked the door. But he felt very calm, just a little tired as he often did in the late afternoon. And he would gladly have asked her permission to lie down on the bed.

He kept repeating a name to himself and could not get it out of his head. Le Tremblay. A racecourse in the south-eastern suburbs where Chantal and Paul had taken him one Sunday in the autumn. Paul had exchanged a few words in the grandstand with a man who was older than them and he had explained to them that this was someone he occasionally used to meet at the casino at Forges-les-Eaux and that he too used to attend race meetings. The man had offered to drive them back to Paris in his car. It was real autumn weather, and not like today's Indian summer, when it was so hot in this room, and he was not at all sure when he would be able to leave . . . She had closed the sky-blue cardboard folder and had laid it on her lap.

"We must go and make photocopies for you . . . It's near here . . ."

She glanced at her watch.

"The shop closes at seven o'clock . . . we've got time . . ."

Later on, he would try to remember the precise year of that particular autumn. From Le Tremblay, they had followed the Marne and crossed the Vincennes woods at dusk. Daragane was sitting next to the man who was driving, the other two in the back. The man had appeared surprised when Paul had introduced them – Jean Daragane.

They spoke about this and that, about the last race at Le Tremblay. The man had said to him:

"Your name's Daragane? I think I met your parents a long time ago . . ."

This term "parents" surprised him. He felt as though he had never had any parents.

"It was about fifteen years ago . . . At a house near Paris . . . I remember a child . . ."

The man had turned towards him.

"The child, it was you, I imagine . . ."

Daragane feared that the man might ask him questions about a period of his life he no longer thought about. And if so, he would not have much to tell him. But he remained silent. After a while, the man asked him:

"I can no longer remember what that place near Paris was . . ."

"Neither can I." And he regretted having answered him in such a curt manner.

Yes, he would eventually recall the precise date of that particular autumn. But for the time being, he was still sitting on the edge of the bed, next to this Chantal, and it seemed to him that he had woken up after suddenly dozing. He tried to pick up the thread of the conversation.

"Do you often wear this dress?"

He pointed to the black satin dress with the two yellow swallows.

"I found it here when I rented the room. It must have belonged to the previous lodger."

"Or perhaps to you, in an earlier life."

She frowned and stared at him suspiciously. She said to him:

"We can go and make the photocopies."

She stood up, and Daragane had the impression that she wished to leave the room as quickly as possible. What was she frightened of? Perhaps he should not have mentioned that dress to her.

WHEN HE GOT BACK HOME, HE WONDERED WHETHER he had not been dreaming. It was probably due to the Indian summer and the heat.

She had dragged him along to a stationery shop on boulevard Voltaire, at the back of which was a photocopier. The typewritten sheets were as flimsy as the paper once used to send letters "by airmail".

They had left the shop and had gone a little way down the boulevard. It was as though she did not want to leave him again. Perhaps she was afraid that once they parted there would be no further sign of him and that Gilles Ottolini might never know who the mysterious Torstel was. But he, too, would be quite happy to remain in her company, so much did the prospect of returning on his own to his apartment make him feel apprehensive.

"If you read the dossier this evening, it may refresh your

memory . . ." and she pointed to the orange cardboard folder that he was holding, which contained the photocopies. She had even insisted that the photograph of the child be reproduced. "You can call me any time tonight . . . Gilles will not be back until tomorrow afternoon. I'd very much like to know what you think of all that . . ."

And she had taken from her wallet a visiting card in the name of Chantal Grippay, with her address, 118 rue de Charonne, and her mobile phone number.

"I must go home now . . . Gilles is going to call me and I've forgotten to take my mobile."

They had made an about-turn and walked in the direction of rue de Charonne. Neither of them said anything. They had no need to talk. She seemed to find it natural that they should walk side by side, and it had occurred to Daragane that if he took her arm she would let him do so, as though they had known one another for a long time. At the staircase to the Charonne métro station, they had gone their separate ways.

Now, in his study, he was leafing through the pages of the "dossier", but he did not feel like reading them immediately.

To begin with, they had been typed without double spacing, and this mass of printed letters piled one on top of the other discouraged him from the start. And then, in the end, he had identified him, this Torstel. On the way back from Le

Tremblay that Sunday in autumn, the man wanted to drop each of them home. But Chantal and Paul had got out at Montparnasse. From there, the métro was direct to where they lived. He stayed in the car because the man had told him that he lived not far from square du Graisivaudan, where he, Daragane, had this room.

They kept silent throughout most of the journey. The man had eventually said to him:

"I must have been to this house near Paris two or three times . . . It was your mother who took me there . . ."

Daragane had not replied. He really did try to avoid thinking about this distant period of his life. And his mother, he did not even know whether she was still alive.

The man had stopped the car by square du Graisivaudan.

"Give my best wishes to your mother . . . We haven't seen one another for a very long time . . . We were part of a kind of club, with some friends . . . the Chrysalis Club . . . Listen, if by any chance she wants to get in touch with me . . ."

He handed him a visiting card on which were written "Guy Torstel" and – as far as he could remember – the address where he worked – a bookshop in the Palais-Royal. And a phone number. Later on, Daragane had lost the visiting card. But he had nevertheless copied out the name and the phone number – why? – in the address book he had at the time.

He sat at his desk. Beneath the pages of the "dossier", he discovered the photocopy of page 47 of his novel, *Le Noir de l'été*, where there was a mention, apparently, of this Torstel. The name was underlined, by Gilles Ottolini no doubt. He read:

> In the Galerie de Beaujolais, there was indeed a bookshop behind whose window some art books were displayed. He went in. A dark-haired woman was sitting at her desk.
>
> "I should like to talk to Monsieur Morihien."
>
> "Monsieur Morihien is away," she told him. "But would you like to speak to Monsieur Torstel?"

That was all. Not much. The name was not mentioned except on page 47 of his novel. And that night he really didn't feel like searching among the typewritten pages without double-spacing of the "Torstel" file. A needle in a haystack.

He recalled that on the lost visiting card there had indeed been the address of a bookshop, in the Palais-Royal. And perhaps the telephone number was that of the bookshop. But after more than forty-five years, these two pathetic details were not enough to set him on the trail of a man who was now no more than a name.

He lay down on the sofa and closed his eyes. He had

decided to make an effort and to take himself back in time, if only for a moment. He had begun the novel, *Le Noir de l'été*, in the autumn, the same autumn when he had gone to Le Tremblay one Sunday. He remembered he had written the first page of the novel that Sunday evening in the room in square du Graisivaudan. A few hours earlier, when Torstel had been driving along the banks of the Marne and then crossed the Vincennes woods, he really had felt affected by autumn: the mist, the smell of damp earth, the paths strewn with dead leaves. The word "Tremblay" would always be associated for him now with that particular autumn.

And so would the name Torstel which he had once used in the novel. Simply because of its resonance. That is what Torstel conjured up for him. There was no need to look any further. It was all he had to say. Gilles Ottolini would no doubt be disappointed. Too bad. After all, he was not obliged to give him any explanation. It was none of his business.

Almost eleven o'clock in the evening. When he was at home on his own at that time, he often experienced what is known as "momentary flagging". Then he would go into a neighbourhood café that stayed open very late at night. The bright light, the hubbub of noise, the comings and goings, the conversations in which he deluded himself he was participating, all this helped him overcome his momentary flagging after a short while. But for some time, he had no longer needed to resort to this expedient. It was enough for him to look out of his study window at the tree planted in the courtyard of the adjoining building, which retained its leaves much later than the others, until November. He had been told that it was a hornbeam, or an aspen, he was not sure. He regretted all the lost years when he had not paid sufficient attention to either the trees or the flowers. He, who no longer read any books other than Buffon's *Histoire naturelle*, suddenly recalled a passage from the memoirs of a French philosopher. She had been shocked by what a woman had said during the war: "After all, the war doesn't alter my relationship with a blade of grass." She probably reckoned that this woman was frivolous or indifferent. But for him, Daragane, the phrase had another meaning: in periods of disaster or mental anxiety, all you need do is look for a fixed point in order to keep your balance and not topple overboard. Your gaze alights on a blade of grass, a tree, the petals of a flower, as though you were clinging on to a buoy. This hornbeam – or this aspen – on the other side of his windowpane reassured him. And even though it was almost eleven o'clock at night, he felt comforted by its silent presence. Therefore, he might as well be done with it straight away and read the typed pages. He had to face the facts: Gilles Ottolini's voice and physique had at first glance struck him as those of a blackmailer. He had wanted to overcome this prejudice. But had he really managed to do so?

He removed the paperclip that held the sheets together. The photocopying paper was not the same as the originals. He remembered when Chantal Grippay was doing the photocopying how flimsy and transparent the pages were. They had reminded him of "airmail" notepaper. But that was not entirely correct. It was rather that they had the same transparency as the onionskin paper used for police interrogations. And besides, Chantal Grippay had told him: "Gilles was able to obtain information from the police . . ."

He cast a last glance at the foliage of the tree, in front of him, before beginning his reading.

The print was tiny, as though it had been typed on one of those portable machines that no longer exist nowadays. Daragane felt as though he was diving into a thick, indigestible broth. Occasionally, he would skip a line and would then have to go back again, with the help of his index finger. Rather than a coherent report, it consisted of some very brief notes, placed end to end in the greatest possible muddle, concerning the murder of a certain Colette Laurent.

The notes retraced her career path. Arrival in Paris when very young from provincial France. Job in a nightclub in rue de Ponthieu. Room in a hotel in the Odéon district. She goes around with students from the École des Beaux-Arts. List of people questioned and whom she may have met in the night club, list of students at the Beaux-Arts. Body found in a hotel bedroom, 15th arrondissement. Interrogation of the owner of the hotel.

So was this the news item that interested Ottolini? He broke off from his reading. Colette Laurent. This apparently anodyne name aroused an echo in him, but too muted for him to be able to describe it. He seemed to have read the date: 1951, but he did not feel like verifying this among the words that were all huddled together and made you feel as if you were suffocating.

1951. More than half a century had gone by since then, and the witnesses to this news item, and even the murderer himself, were no longer alive. Gilles Ottolini had got there too late. This shit-stirrer would be left unsatisfied. Daragane regretted that he had described him in such a crude way. A few more pages to go. He still experienced this nervousness and this apprehension that had come over him when he had opened the "dossier".

He gazed for a moment at the leaves of the hornbeam, which were quivering gently, as though the tree was breathing in its sleep. Yes, this tree was his friend, and he recalled the title of a collection of poems an eight-year-old girl had had published: *Arbre, mon ami.* He was jealous of this girl, because he had been the same age as her and because he, too, wrote poems at the time. What period did this date from? From a year during his childhood almost as long ago as the year 1951 in the course of which Colette Laurent had been murdered.

Once again, the tiny letters without double-spacing danced before his eyes. And he had to slide his forefinger along so as not to lose the thread. At last, the name Guy Torstel. It was linked to three names among which he was surprised to recognise that of his mother. The two others were: Bob Bugnand and Jacques Perrin de Lara. He vaguely remembered them, and this too went back to the distant period when the girl of his own age had published *Arbre, mon ami.* The first one, Bugnand, had the figure of a sportsman and wore beige. Dark-haired, he believed; and the other, a man with the large head of a Roman statue, who perched his elbow on marble fireplaces in an elegant pose when he spoke. Childhood memories often consist of small, trivial details that come from nowhere. Had these names attracted Ottolini's attention and had he made a connection between them and he himself, Daragane? But no, certainly not. Firstly, his mother did not use the same surname as he did. The two others, Bugnand and Perrin de Lara, were lost in the mists of time, and Ottolini was too young for them to mean anything to him.

The more he read, the more he had the sense that this "dossier" was a sort of ragbag in which bits and pieces from two different investigations that had not taken place in the same year had been thrown together, since the date was now given as 1952. However, between the notes from 1951 dealing with the murder of Colette Laurent and those on the two last pages, he thought he could detect a slender unifying thread: "Colette Laurent" had visited "a house in Saint-Leu-la-Forêt" where "a certain Annie Astrand" lived. This house was apparently under police supervision – but for what reason? Among the names mentioned, those of Torstel, his mother, Bugnand and Perrin de Lara. Two other names were not unknown to him. Roger Vincent and in particular that of the woman who lived in the house at Saint-Leu-la-Forêt, "a certain Annie Astrand".

He would have liked to put these muddled notes into some sort of order, but this seemed beyond his powers. What is more, at this late hour of the night, one often comes up with some peculiar notions: the target whom Gilles Ottolini had in mind when he had gathered all the notes in his file, well it was not some old news item, but he himself, Daragane. Of course, Ottolini had not found the angle to fire from, he groped around, he got lost along crossed paths, he was incapable of reaching the heart of the matter. Daragane could sense him prowling around him in search of a way in. Perhaps he had gathered together all these disparate elements in the hope that Daragane would react to one of them, like those police officers who begin an interrogation with petty remarks in order to lull the suspect's defences. Then, when the person feels safe, they suddenly fire the crucial question at him.

His eyes settled once more on the leaves of the hornbeam tree and he felt ashamed of such notions. He was losing his composure. The few pages he had just read were merely an inept draft, an accumulation of details that concealed what was most important. One name alone disturbed him and drew him like a magnet: Annie Astrand. But it was barely legible amid these words jumbled together without double-spacing. Annie Astrand. A faraway voice picked up late at night on the radio and you persuade yourself that she is speaking to you in order to give you a message. Someone had told him one day that you forget the voices of those whom you have been close to in the past very quickly. Yet if he were to hear the voice of Annie Astrand today, in the street, he was certain he would recognise it.

When he was next in Ottolini's company, he would be very careful not to draw attention to this name: Annie Astrand, but he was not sure whether he would see him again. If need be, he would write a very brief note to give him the sparse information about Guy Torstel. A man who looked after a bookshop in the Galerie de Beaujolais, adjoining the Palais-Royal gardens. Yes, he had met him only once, almost fifty years ago, one Sunday evening in autumn at Le Tremblay. He could even carry kindness a step further by providing him with a few additional details about the two others, Bugnand and Perrin de Lara. Friends of his mother, as Guy Torstel must have been. In the year when he read the poems in *Arbre, mon ami* and when he felt envious of that girl of his own age who was the author, Bugnand and Perrin de Lara – and perhaps Torstel too – always carried a book in their pocket, like a missal, a book to which they appeared to attach great importance. He remembered its title: *Fabrizio Lupo*. One day, Perrin de Lara had said to him in a solemn voice: "When you're grown up, you too will read *Fabrizio Lupo*", one of those remarks that will continue to sound mysterious until the end of one's life, because of its resonance. Later on, he had searched for this book, but unfortunately he had never found a copy of it and he had never read *Fabrizio Lupo*. He would not need to bring up these minute recollections. The likeliest outcome was that he would eventually be rid of Gilles Ottolini. Telephone calls that he would not answer. Letters, some of which would be registered. Most annoying of all would be that Ottolini would station himself outside the building and, since he did not know the code, he would wait for someone to push open the porte cochère and slip in behind him. He would come and ring at his door. He would also have to disconnect this bell. Every time he left his home, he would run into Gilles Ottolini who would accost him and follow him in the street. And he would have no alternative but to take refuge in the nearest police station. But the cops would not take his explanations seriously.

It was almost one o'clock in the morning, and he reckoned that at that time of day, in the silence and solitude, one begins to worry unduly. He gradually calmed down, and even burst out into a fit of mad laughter at the thought of Ottolini's face, one of those faces that are so narrow that even when they are standing opposite you, you would think they were in profile.

The typed pages were scattered over his desk. He picked up a pencil that had red lead at one end and blue lead at the other, which he used to correct his manuscripts. He scored through the pages with the blue pencil as he went along and he drew a circle in red round the name: ANNIE ASTRAND.

AT ABOUT TWO O'CLOCK IN THE MORNING, THE TELE-
phone rang. He had fallen asleep on the sofa.

"Hello . . . Monsieur Daragane? This is Chantal Grippay . . ."

He hesitated for a moment. He had just had a dream in
which Annie Astrand's face had appeared to him, and that had
not happened to him for more than thirty or so years.

"You've read the photocopies?"

"Yes."

"Forgive me for phoning so late . . . but I was so eager for
you to give me your opinion . . . Can you hear me?"

"Yes."

"We must see one another before Gilles returns. May I call
at your home?"

"Now?"

"Yes. Now."

He told her the address, the entry code, the floor. Had he

surfaced from his dream? Annie Astrand's face had seemed so close a moment ago . . . She was at the wheel of her car, outside the house at Saint-Leu-la-Forêt, he was sitting on the front seat beside her, and she was speaking to him, but he could not hear the sound of her voice.

On his desk, the photocopies, in a muddle. He had forgotten that he had scored blue lines through them. And the name: Annie Astrand, which leapt out at you, because it was circled in red . . . He would have to avoid showing that to Gilles Ottolini. This red circle might give him a lead. Any cop would have put the question if he had come across it, after slowly leafing through the pages.

"Why have you highlighted this name?"

He glanced over at the hornbeam whose leaves were motionless, and this reassured him. This tree was a sentry, the only person who watched over him. He went and stood at the window overlooking the street. No cars went by at this time and the streetlamps gleamed pointlessly. He saw Chantal Grippay who was walking along the pavement on the opposite side, and she seemed to be looking at the numbers of the buildings. She was holding a plastic bag in her hand. He wondered whether she had walked here from rue de Charonne. He heard the porte cochère shutting suddenly and her footsteps on the staircase, a very slow footstep, as though she were hesitating to come up. Before she rang the bell, he opened the door and she gave a start. She was still wearing a black blouse and black trousers. She seemed to him as shy as she had been the first time, at the café on rue de l'Arcade.

"I didn't want to disturb you so late . . ."

She stood at the doorstep with an apologetic air, not moving. He took her arm to lead her in. Otherwise, he had the feeling that she would have done an about-turn. In the room he used as a study, he pointed her to the sofa where she sat down, and she placed her plastic bag beside her.

"So, have you read it?"

She had asked the question in an anxious tone of voice. Why did she attach such importance to it?

"I've read it, but I can't really be of any help to your friend. I don't know these people."

"Even Torstel?"

She looked him straight in the eyes.

The interrogation would start again, without interruption, until the morning. Then, at about eight o'clock, the doorbell would ring. It would be Gilles Ottolini, back from Lyon, who would come and take over from her.

"Yes, even Torstel."

"Why use this name in a book, if you hadn't known him?"

She had adopted a falsely naive tone.

"I choose names at random, by looking at the telephone directory."

"So, you can't help Gilles."

He came and sat down beside her on the sofa and brought his face closer to hers. Once again, he saw the scar on her left cheekbone.

"He wants you to help him write . . . He thought that you were very closely involved with everything noted down in these papers . . ."

At that moment, he had the feeling that the roles were being reversed and that it would not take much to "crack" her, according to the expression he had once heard among a particular milieu. Beneath the glow of the lamp, he noticed the rings under her eyes and the quivering of her hands. She seemed to him paler than she had a moment ago, when he had opened the door to her.

On his desk, the pages that he had struck through in blue pencil were clearly visible. But for the time being she had not noticed anything.

"Gilles has read all your books and he has made enquiries about you . . ."

These words made him feel slightly uneasy. He had had the misfortune to attract the attention of someone who would not let go of him from now on. Rather like certain people whose eyes meet yours. They can suddenly be hostile without the slightest reason, or else they come up and speak to you, and it is very difficult to get rid of them. He always tried to lower his gaze in the street.

"And then, they're intending to make him redundant at the Sweerts agency . . . He's going to find himself unemployed once again . . ."

Daragane was struck by the weary tone her voice had taken on. He thought he could detect a note of exasperation in this weariness, and even a slight contempt.

"He thought you were going to help him . . . He has the feeling that he's known you for a long time . . . He knows a lot about you . . ."

She seemed to want to say more. It would soon be the time of night when the make-up starts to run and you are on the brink of revealing secrets.

"Would you care for something to drink?"

"Oh yes . . . something strong . . . I need a fillip . . ."

Daragane was amazed that at her age she should use this outmoded expression. He had not heard the word "fillip" for a long time. Perhaps Annie Astrand used it in the old days. She held her hands clasped together, as though she were trying to stop them shaking.

In the kitchen cupboard, all he could find was a half-empty

bottle of vodka and he wondered who could possibly have left it there. She had settled herself on the sofa, her legs out-stretched, her back leaning against the big orange cushion.

"I'm sorry, but I'm feeling a bit tired . . ."

She gulped a mouthful down. Then another.

"That's better. They're dreadful, these kinds of parties . . ."

She looked at Daragane, as though she wished to call him as a witness. He paused for a moment before asking her the question.

"What parties?"

"The one I've just come from . . ."

Then, in a brusque voice:

"I'm paid to go to these 'parties' . . . it's because of Gilles . . . He needs money . . ."

She lowered her head. She seemed to regret her remarks. She turned to Daragane, sitting opposite her on the green velvet stool.

"It's not him you should be helping . . . it's me . . ."

She shot him a smile that could have been described as weak or wan.

"I'm a decent girl, all the same . . . So, I ought to warn you about Gilles . . ."

She adjusted her position and sat on the edge of the sofa so as to be right in front of him.

"He's learnt some things about you . . . through this friend in the police . . . So, he was trying to get in touch with you . . ."

Tiredness? Daragane no longer understood what she was saying. What could the "things" that this person had learnt about him from the police actually be? In any case, the pages from the "dossier" were not very conclusive. And he scarcely knew any of the names cited. Apart from his mother, Torstel, Bugnand and Perrin de Lara. But from so long ago . . . They had mattered so little in his life . . . Walk-on parts, long since dead. Of course, Annie Astrand was mentioned. Briefly. Her name went completely unnoticed, it was lost among the others. And on one occasion, with a spelling mistake: Astran.

"Don't worry on my behalf," Daragane said. "I'm not frightened of anyone. And especially not blackmailers."

She seemed surprised that he should have used this term: blackmailer, but as though it were something obvious that she had not thought of.

"I always wondered whether he hadn't stolen your address book from you . . ."

She smiled, and Daragane thought that she had meant this as a joke.

"Sometimes, Gilles frightens me . . . That's why I stay with him . . . We've known each other for such a long time . . ."

The voice was more and more hoarse, and he feared that

this confiding of secrets might go on until morning. Could he maintain his attention and listen until it was over?

"He didn't go to Lyon for his work, but to gamble at the casino..."

"The casino at Charbonnières?"

The phrase had come to his lips very quickly, and he was surprised by the word "Charbonnières", which he had forgotten and which now came back again from the past. When they had set off to go gambling at the casino at Charbonnières, Paul and the others left on the Friday in the early afternoon, and they returned to Paris on the Monday. So, that meant almost three days spent with Chantal at the room in square du Graisivaudan.

"Yes, he went to the casino at Charbonnières. He knows a croupier down there... He always returns from the casino at Charbonnières with a little more money than usual."

"And you don't go with him?"

"Never. Except at the beginning, when we first knew one another... I used to wait for him for hours at the Cercle Gaillon... There was a waiting room for the women..."

Had Daragane misunderstood? "Gaillon" – like "Charbonnières" – was a name that he was familiar with in the past. Chantal used to join him unexpectedly in the room in square du Graisivaudan and would say to him: "Paul's at the Cercle

Gaillon . . . We can spend the evening together . . . And even the night . . ."

So, did the Cercle Gaillon still exist? Unless the same ridiculous words that you have heard in your youth return like an old tune or a stammer, many years later and towards the end of your life?

"When I am on my own in Paris, they make me join in slightly unusual parties . . . I accept because of Gilles . . . He always needs money . . . And now it will be worse because he'll find himself without a job . . ."

Yet how had he come to be on close terms with Gilles Ottolini and this Chantal Grippay? In the past, new encounters were often blunt and frank – two people who collide with one another in the street, like the bumper cars of his childhood. Here, everything had happened gently, a lost address book, voices on the telephone, a meeting in a café . . . Yes, it all had the lightness of a dream. And the pages of the "dossier" had also given him a strange sensation: because of certain names, and especially that of Annie Astrand, and all those words piled on top of each other without double-spacing, he suddenly found himself confronted with certain details of his life, but reflected in a distorting mirror, with those disjointed details that pursue you on nights when you have a temperature.

"He's coming back from Charbonnières tomorrow . . . at

about midday . . . He'll be pestering you again . . . Whatever you do, don't tell him we've seen each other."

Daragane wondered whether she was being honest and whether she might not let Ottolini know about her visit to him that night. Unless it could have been Ottolini who had asked her to carry out this assignment. In any case, he was sure of being able to get rid of them sooner or later, as he had done with many people during the course of his life.

"In short," he said cheerfully, "you're a couple of criminals."

She appeared astounded by these words. He regretted them immediately. She was hunched up and for a moment he thought she was about to dissolve into tears. He leant over towards her, but she avoided his gaze.

"All this, it's because of Gilles . . . I had nothing to do with it . . ."

Then, after a moment's hesitation:

"Be careful of him . . . He'll want to see you every day . . . He won't give you a moment's peace . . . The guy is . . ."

" . . . clinging?"

"Yes. Very clinging."

And she seemed to give this term a more worrying significance than he had first intended.

"I don't know what he has learnt about you . . . Perhaps

something in the dossier . . . I haven't read it . . . He'll use it as a means of putting pressure . . ."

The words she had just used sounded false coming from her. It was doubtless Ottolini who had spoken to her about a "means of putting pressure".

"He wants you to help him write a book . . . That's what he told me . . ."

"Are you sure he doesn't want anything else?"

She hesitated for a moment.

"No."

"Perhaps ask me for money?"

"It's possible . . . Gamblers need money . . . Yes, of course he's going to ask you for money . . ."

They must have discussed the matter after the meeting in rue de l'Arcade. They probably had their backs to the wall – an expression that Chantal used to employ in the past, when she spoke about Paul. But he always thought he would recover thanks to his doubling up on his losses.

"Soon, he won't even be able to pay the rent for his room in square du Graisivaudan . . ."

Yes, rents had certainly increased over forty-five years in square du Graisivaudan. Daragane occupied the room illegally, thanks to a friend to whom the owner had entrusted the keys. There was a telephone in this room, with a padlock on the dial so that no-one could use it. But he succeeded in dialling certain numbers all the same.

"I, too," he said, "lived in square du Graisivaudan . . ."

She looked at him in surprise, as if she were discovering links between them. He was on the point of adding that the girl who occasionally came to join him in this room was also called Chantal. But what was the point? She said to him:

"Well, perhaps it's the same room that Gilles has . . . An attic room . . . you take the lift and then go up a small staircase . . ."

Yes, that was right, the lift did not go to the top floor – a corridor with a succession of rooms along it, each with a partially faded number on the door. His was number 5. He remembered because of Paul, who often tried to explain to him one of his formulas for doubling up on his losses "around the neutral five".

"And I had a friend who gambled at the races, and also went to the casino at Charbonnières . . ."

She seemed reassured by these words and she gave him a faint smile. She must have thought that even though there were a few dozen years between them they came from the same world. But which one?

"So, you were coming back from one of your parties?"

He immediately regretted asking her the question. But she

evidently felt she could trust him:

"Yes . . . It's a couple who organise rather special parties in their apartment . . . Gilles worked for them for a while as chauffeur . . . They used to phone me from time to time to get me to come . . . It's Gilles who wants me to go . . . They pay me . . . I can't do anything else . . ."

He listened to her without daring to interrupt. Perhaps her remarks were not meant for him and she had forgotten he was there. It must be very late. Five in the morning? Daybreak would soon come and would scatter the shadows. He would find himself alone in his study after a bad dream. No, he had never lost this address book. Neither Gilles Ottolini nor Joséphine Grippay who called herself Chantal had ever existed.

"It's going to be very difficult for you, too, to get rid of Gilles now . . . He won't let you go . . . I wouldn't put it past him to wait for you at the door of your building . . ."

A threat or a warning? With dreams, thought Daragane, one is never really certain what they're to do with. A dream? All would become clear at daybreak. And yet sitting here, opposite him, there was nothing ghostly about her. He was not sure whether voices could be heard in dreams, but he could hear Chantal Grippay's husky voice very clearly.

"I've got one piece of advice for you: don't answer his phone calls anymore . . ."

She was leaning towards him and speaking in a very low voice, as though Gilles Ottolini were standing behind the door.

"You must leave messages for me on my mobile . . . When he's no longer there, I'll call you back . . . I'll keep you informed about what he's planning to do. In that way, you'll be able to avoid him . . ."

This girl was clearly very considerate, but Daragane would have liked to explain to her that he could cope on his own. He had come across other Ottolinis in his life. He knew a great many buildings in Paris that had two entrances, and thanks to them he was able to shake people off. And so as to make people think that he had gone out, he often kept the lights switched off at home, because of the two windows that overlooked the street.

"I lent you a book and told you that Gilles had written it . . . *Le Flâneur hippique* . . ."

He had forgotten the existence of this book. He had left it in the orange cardboard folder when he took out the photocopies.

"It's not true . . . Gilles makes people think he wrote this book because its author has the same name as him . . . but not the same first name . . . And, what's more, the guy's dead . . ."

She rummaged in the plastic bag that she had put down beside her on the sofa. From it, she brought out the black satin dress with two yellow swallows that Daragane had noticed in her room in rue de Charonne.

"I forgot my pair of high-heeled shoes at these people's place . . ."

"I know that dress," Daragane said.

"Each time I go to these people's parties, they want me to wear it."

"Odd sort of dress . . ."

"I found it at the bottom of an old cupboard in my room . . . There's a label on the back."

She handed him the dress and on the label he read: "Silvy-Rosa. Fashion design. Rue Estelle. Marseille."

"Perhaps you wore it in an earlier life . . ."

He had said the same thing to her, yesterday afternoon, in the room in rue de Charonne.

"Do you think so?"

"A feeling . . . because of the label, which is very old . . ."

She in turn looked at the label suspiciously. Then she put down the dress, beside her, on the sofa.

"Wait . . . I'm coming back . . ."

He left the study to ascertain whether he had left the light on in the kitchen. The window there overlooked the street. Yes, he had left the light on. He switched it off and stood by the window. A moment ago, he had imagined that Ottolini was keeping watch outside. Such thoughts come to you very late, when you have not slept, thoughts that you once had long ago, as a child, that frighten you. No-one. But he could be hiding behind the fountain or, on the right, behind one of the trees in the square.

He stood there for a long time, very upright, his arms folded. He saw nobody in the street. No cars went by. Had he opened the window, he would have heard the murmur of the fountain and he would have wondered whether he was not in Rome rather than Paris. Rome, from where a long time ago he had received a postcard from Annie Astrand, the last sign of life he had had of her.

When he returned to his study, she was stretched out on the sofa, clad in that strange black satin dress with two yellow swallows. He was confused for a moment. Was she wearing that dress when he had opened the door to her? No, she was not. Her shirt and black trousers were rolled up in a ball on the floor, next to her slip-on shoes. Her eyes were closed and she was breathing steadily. Was she pretending to be asleep?

She had left at about midday and Daragane was alone, as usual, in his study. She was worried that Gilles Ottolini might be back already. When he went to the casino in Charbonnières, he sometimes caught the train for Paris very early on the

Monday morning. Through the window, he had watched her walk away wearing her shirt and her black trousers. She was not carrying the plastic bag. She had left it behind on the sofa along with the dress. It took Daragane a long time before he found the visiting card she had given him, a faded paper visiting card. But the mobile telephone number did not answer. She would surely ring him back in due course, as soon as she noticed that she had forgotten the dress.

He took it out of the bag and looked at the label again: "Silvy-Rosa. Fashion design. Rue Estelle. Marseille". This reminded him of something, even though he had never been to Marseille. He had read this address before, or else heard the name. When he was younger, this type of apparently insignificant mystery could keep him busy for several days during which he searched stubbornly for a solution. Even if it were a matter of a tiny detail, he experienced a feeling of anxiety and privation for as long as he failed to make the connection, rather like a piece of a jigsaw puzzle that has been lost. Sometimes, it was a phrase or a line of verse for which he wanted to find the author, sometimes, a simple name. "Silvy-Rosa. Fashion design. Rue Estelle. Marseille". He closed his eyes and tried to concentrate. Two words came to mind that seemed to be associated with this label: "La Chinoise". It would require the patience of a deep-sea diver to discover the link between

"Silvy-Rosa" and "La Chinoise", but for several years he had no longer had the strength to devote himself to this type of exploit. No, he was too old, he preferred to float along calmly . . . "La Chinoise" . . . Was it on account of this Chantal Grippay's black hair and slightly slanted eyes?

He sat down at his desk. That night, she had not noticed the scattered pages and the deletions in blue pencil. He opened the cardboard folder that he had left by the telephone and took out the book that was inside it. He started to leaf through *Le Flâneur hippique*. It was a recent reprint of a book whose copyright dated from before the war. How could Gilles Ottolini have the cheek, or the naivety, to claim to be its author? He closed the book and glanced at the sheets of paper in front of him. During his first reading, he had skipped sentences because the letters were too cramped together.

Once again, the words danced. There were clearly other details relating to Annie Astrand, but he felt too tired to take them in. He would do so later, in the afternoon, when he had had a rest. Or else he might decide to tear up the pages, one by one. Yes, he would see about that later.

Just as he was putting the "dossier" back in its cardboard folder, his eyes fell on the photograph of the child, which he had forgotten about. On the back of it, he read: "3 passport photos. Unidentified child. Search and arrest Astrand, Annie.

Customs post Ventimiglia. Monday, 21 July 1952." Yes, it was indeed the enlargement of a passport photograph, as he had thought yesterday afternoon in the room in rue de Charonne.

He could not keep his eyes off this photograph and he wondered why he had forgotten it among the sheets in the "dossier". Was it something that embarrassed him, an exhibit, to use the legal language, and which he, Daragane, had wanted to erase from his memory? He experienced a sort of giddiness, a tingling sensation at the roots of his hair. This child, so detached from him over such a very long time to the extent that he had become a stranger, was, he was forced to acknowledge, himself.

DURING A DIFFERENT AUTUMN TO THAT SUNDAY at Le Tremblay, an autumn equally long ago, Daragane had received a letter at square du Graisivaudan. He was walking past the concierge's door just as she was about to distribute the post.

"I suppose you're Jean Daragane." And she handed him a letter that had his name written in blue ink on the envelope. He had never received any post at this address. He did not recognise the handwriting, a very large handwriting that covered the entire envelope: Jean Daragane, 8 square du Graisivaudan, Paris. There was not enough space for the number of the arrondissement. On the back of the envelope, a name and an address: A. Astrand, 18 rue Alfred-Dehodencq, Paris.

For a few seconds, this name did not register with him at all. Was it because of the simple initial "A" that concealed the first name? Later on, he reckoned that he had had a premonition because he hesitated to open the letter. He walked to the boundary between Neuilly and Levallois, through that area where, in two or three years' time, the garages and humble houses would be torn down to build the ring road. ASTRAND. How could he not have realised, in that very instant, whom it referred to?

He turned around and walked into the café beneath one of the blocks of flats. He sat down, took the letter out of his pocket, asked for an orange juice, and, if possible, a knife. He opened the letter with the knife, because he feared that if he used his hands he might tear the address on the back of the envelope. All it contained were three passport photos. In all three, he recognised himself as a child. He remembered the afternoon on which they had been taken, in a shop, the other side of the pont Saint-Michel, opposite the Palais de Justice. Since then, he had often walked past this shop, exactly as it was in the old days.

He needed to find these passport photos to compare them with the enlargement that was part of Ottolini's "file". In the suitcase in which he had crammed letters and papers that were at least forty years old and to which he had, fortunately, lost the key? No point. They were certainly the same photographs. "Unidentified child. Search and arrest Astrand, Annie. Customs post Ventimiglia. Monday 21 July 1952." They must have arrested and searched her at the very moment she was preparing to cross the frontier.

She had read his novel, *Le Noir de l'été* and she had recognised an episode from that particular summer. Otherwise, why would she have written to him after fifteen years? But how could she have known his temporary address? Especially since he rarely slept at square du Graisivaudan. He spent the greater part of his time in a room in rue Coustou and in the place Blanche neighbourhood.

He had written this book only in the hope that she might get in touch with him. Writing a book, for him, was also a way of beaming a searchlight or sending out coded signals to certain people with whom he had lost touch. It was enough to scatter their names at random through the pages and wait until they finally produced news of themselves. But in the case of Annie Astrand, he had not mentioned her name and he had endeavoured to cover his tracks. She would not be able to recognise herself in any of his characters. He had never understood why anyone should want to put someone who had mattered to them into a novel. Once that person had drifted into a novel in much the same way as one might walk through a mirror, he escaped from you forever. He had never existed in real life. He had been reduced to nothingness . . . You needed to go about it in a more subtle way. For example, in *Le Noir de l'été*, the only page in the book that might attract Annie Astrand's attention was the scene in which the woman and the child walk into the shop with the instant-photo Photomaton booth, on the boulevard du Palais. He does not understand why she pushes him into the booth. She tells him to stare into the screen and not to move his head. She draws the black curtain. He is sitting on the stool. A flash blinds him and he closes his eyes. She draws the black curtain again, and he leaves the booth. They wait for the photos to fall from the slot. And he has to do it all over again because his eyes are shut in the photos. Afterwards, she had taken him to have a grenadine at the nearby café. That was what had happened. He had described the scene precisely and he knew that this passage did not fit with the rest of the novel. It was a fragment of reality that he had smuggled in, one of those private messages that people put in small ads in newspapers and that can only be deciphered by one person.

TOWARDS THE END OF THE AFTERNOON, HE WAS surprised not to have received a phone call from Chantal Grippay. Yet she must have noticed that she had forgotten her black dress. He rang her mobile number, but there was no answer. After the signal, there was silence. You had reached the edge of a cliff beyond which there was nothing but empty space. He wondered whether the number was still functioning or whether Chantal Grippay might have lost her mobile. Or whether she was still alive.

As if by contagion, a doubt arose in his mind concerning Gilles Ottolini. He typed out on the keyboard of his computer: "Agence Sweerts, Paris". No Sweerts agency in Paris, neither in the gare Saint-Lazare area nor in any other district. The supposed author of *Le Flâneur hippique* was merely a bogus employee of an imaginary agency.

He wanted to know if an Ottolini was listed in square du

Graisivaudan, but among the names that featured at the eight numbers of the square, not a single Ottolini. In any case, the black dress was there, on the back of the sofa, proof that he had not been dreaming. He typed out, on the off-chance, "Silvy-Rosa. Fashion design. Rue Estelle. Marseille", but all he obtained was: "Rosa Alterations, 18 rue du Sauvage, 68100 Mulhouse". For the past few years, he hardly ever used this computer on which most of his research came to nothing. The rare people whom he would have liked to trace had succeeded in escaping the vigilance of this machine. They had slipped through the net because they belonged to another age and because they were not exactly saints. He remembered his father whom he hardly knew and who used to say to him in a soft voice: "I'd be a tough case for dozens of examining magistrates." No trace of his father on the computer. Any more than of Torstel or Perrin de Lara whose names he had typed out on the keyboard the previous day, before Chantal Grippay arrived. In the case of Perrin de Lara, the usual phenomenon had occurred: a great many Perrins were displayed on the screen, and the night was not long enough to go through the entire list. Those whom he would have liked to hear from were often hidden among a crowd of anonymous people, or else behind a famous character who bore the same name. And when he typed out a direct question on the keyboard: "Is Jacques Perrin de Lara still alive? If so, give me his address", the computer seemed incapable of replying and you could sense a certain hesitation and a certain embarrassment passing through the multiple wires that connected the machine to electrical sockets. Sometimes, you were dragged off on false trails: "Astrand" produced results in Sweden, and several people of this name were grouped together in the city of Gothenburg.

The weather was hot and this Indian summer would probably extend into November. He decided to go out instead of waiting in his study until sunset, as he usually did. Later on, when he returned, he would try to decipher with the aid of a magnifying glass the photocopies that he had read through too quickly the previous day. Perhaps in this way he would have the opportunity to learn something about Annie Astrand. He regretted not having asked her these questions when he had seen her again fifteen years after the Photomaton shop episode, but he had very soon realised that he would not receive any response from her.

Outside, he felt more carefree than he had on previous days. He may have been wrong to immerse himself in this distant past. What was the point? He had not thought about it for a number of years, and so eventually it seemed to him that he saw this period of his life through a frosted window. It allowed a vague clarity to filter through, but you could not make out the faces or even the figures. A glazed window, a sort of protective screen. Perhaps, thanks to deliberate forgetfulness, he had managed to protect himself from this past for good. Or else, it was time that had subdued its more intense colours and rough edges.

There, on the pavement, in the light of the Indian summer that lent the Paris streets a timeless softness, he once again had the feeling that he was floating on his back. He had not experienced this sensation since last year, and he wondered whether it might not be linked to the onset of old age. When he was very young, he had known those moments of semi-slumber when you allow yourself to drift – usually after being up all night – but today it was different: the sense of free-wheeling down a slope, when the motor has stopped. How far would you go?

He glided, swept along by a breeze and by his own weight. He bumped into pedestrians who were coming in the opposite direction and had not moved out of the way quickly enough as he passed by. He apologised. It was not his fault. Normally, he displayed far greater vigilance when he walked in the street, ready to change pavements if he saw someone in the distance whom he knew or who might accost him. He was aware that you very seldom met anyone you really had wanted to meet. Twice or three times in a lifetime?

He would happily have walked to rue de Charonne to take Chantal Grippay's dress back to her, but he risked coming across Gilles Ottolini. And if he did? It would provide an opportunity to be better informed about the uncertain existence of this man. Chantal Grippay's remark came back to him: "They want to make him redundant at the Sweerts agency." Yet she must know that the Sweerts agency did not exist. And the book, Le Flâneur hippique, the copyright of which dated from before the war? Had Ottolini taken the manuscript to Éditions du Sablier in a former life and under a different first name? He, Daragane, deserved a few explanations about these matters, after all.

He had reached the arcades of the Palais-Royal. He had walked without any particular aim. But, in crossing the Pont des Arts and the courtyard of the Louvre, he was following a route that was familiar to him from his childhood. He walked along what is known as the Louvre des Antiquaires and he remembered the Christmas windows of the Grands Magasins du Louvre in the same spot. And now that he had paused in the middle of the Galerie de Beaujolais, as though he had reached the end of his walk, another memory came back to him. It had been buried away for so long and so deeply, far from the light of day, that it seemed new. He wondered whether it really was a memory or whether it was a snapshot that no longer belonged to the past, having detached itself like a free electron: his mother and he – one of the rare occasions when they were together – entering a shop that sold books and paintings, and his mother speaking to two men, one of whom was sitting at a desk at the back of the shop while the other stood with his elbow propped against a marble fireplace. Guy Torstel. Jacques Perrin de Lara. Frozen there, until the end of time. How could it be that on that Sun-day in autumn when he had returned from Le Tremblay with Chantal and Paul, in Torstel's car, this name should not have reminded him of anything, any more than his visiting card did, despite the fact that the address of the shop was printed on it?

In the car, Torstel had even referred to "the house on the outskirts of Paris" where, as a child, he had seen him at Annie Astrand's house. He, Daragane, had stayed there for almost a year. At Saint-Leu-la-Forêt. "I remember a child," Torstel had said. "That child was you, I suppose . . ." And Daragane had replied to him curtly, as though this was nothing to do with him. It was the Sunday when he had begun to write *Le Noir de l'été* after Torstel had dropped him at square du Graisivaudan. And not for a moment had he had the presence of mind to ask him whether he remembered the woman who lived in this house, at Saint-Leu-la-Forêt, "a certain Annie Astrand". And whether he happened to know what had become of her.

He sat down on a garden bench, in the sunshine, near the arcades of the Galerie de Beaujolais. He must have walked for over an hour without even noticing that it was hotter still than on the other days. Torstel. Perrin de Lara. But yes, he had met Perrin de Lara one final time, in the same year as that Sunday at Le Tremblay – he was barely twenty-one – and this meeting would have vanished into *la nuit froide de l'oubli* – as the song goes – had it not been to do with Annie Astrand. One evening, he happened to be in a café on the Rond-Point des Champs-Élysées, one that had been converted into a "Drugstore" in the years that followed. It was ten o'clock. A pause before continuing his walk to square du Graisivaudan, or rather to a room in rue Coustou that he had been renting for some time at six hundred francs a month.

He had not immediately noticed the presence, that night, of Perrin de Lara, in front of him, sitting on the terrace. Alone.

Why had he spoken to him? He had not seen him for over ten years, and this man would certainly not recognise him. But he was writing his first book, and Annie Astrand was filling his mind in an obsessive way. Perhaps Perrin de Lara knew something about her?

He had stood in front of his table, and the man had looked up. No, he did not recognise him.

"Jean Daragane."

"Ah . . . Jean . . ."

He smiled at him, a faint smile, as though he were embarrassed that someone should recognise him at that time of night, on his own, in such a place.

"You've grown taller over the years . . . Sit down, Jean . . ."

He pointed to the chair, opposite him. Daragane hesitated for a fraction of a second. The glazed terrace door was ajar. All he had to do was say what he normally said: "Wait . . . I'll be back . . ." Then go out into the open air of the night, and take a deep breath. And, most importantly, avoid any further contact with a shadow, who would be waiting over there, alone, on a café terrace, for all eternity.

He sat down. Perrin de Lara's Roman-statue face had become bloated and his hair had acquired a greyish tinge. He was wearing a navy-blue linen jacket that was too flimsy for the season. In front of him, a half-drunk glass of Martini, which Daragane recognised by its colour.

"And your mother? It's years since I've been in touch with her . . . You know . . . we were like brother and sister . . ."

He shrugged, and there was an anxious expression in his eyes.

"I've been away from Paris for a long time . . ."

It was clear that he would have liked to tell him about the reasons for this long absence. But he remained silent.

"And have you seen your friends Torstel and Bob Bugnand again?"

Perrin de Lara seemed surprised to hear these two names coming from Daragane's lips. Surprised, and suspicious.

"What a memory you have . . . do you remember those two? . . ."

He stared at Daragane, whose gaze made him feel uncomfortable.

"No . . . I don't see them anymore . . . It's incredible what good memories children have . . . And you, what's new?"

Daragane could sense a note of bitterness in this question. But perhaps he was mistaken, or else in Perrin de Lara's case was it simply the effect of a Martini drunk on his own, at ten o'clock at night, in autumn, on the terrace of a café?

"I'm trying to write a book . . ."

He wondered why he had admitted this.

"Ah . . . like the time when you were jealous of Minou Drouet?"

Daragane had forgotten this name. But yes, this was the little girl of his own age who had once published the anthology of poems, *Arbre, mon ami.*

82

"Literature's a very difficult thing . . . I suppose you must have realised this already . . ."

Perrin de Lara's voice had taken on a moralising tone that surprised Daragane. The little he knew of him and the childhood memory he retained of him would have led him to think that this man was rather frivolous. The sort of person who perches his elbow on marble fireplaces. Had he, like his mother and Torstel, and possibly Bob Bugnand too, belonged to the "Chrysalis Club"?

He eventually said to him:

"So, after all this time away, you've come back to Paris for good?"

The man shrugged and looked at Daragane with a haughty expression, as though the latter had lacked respect.

"I don't know what you mean by 'for good'."

Daragane did not know either. He had simply said that for the sake of conversation. And the man was very touchy . . . He felt like standing up and saying to him: "Well, good luck, monsieur . . ." and, before going through the glazed terrace door, he would smile and wave to him, as though on a railway station platform. He restrained himself. Patience was required. He may know something about Annie Astrand.

"You used to give me advice about reading . . . Do you remember?"

He did his best to speak with emotion. And it was true, after all, that when he was a child this shadowy figure had given him La Fontaine's *Fables* in the Classiques Hachette collection with their pale green covers. And some time later, the same man had recommended that he read *Fabrizio Lupo* when he was older.

"You really do have a good memory . . ."

His tone had softened, and Perrin de Lara was smiling at him. But the smile was slightly strained. He leant over towards Daragane:

"I have to tell you . . . I no longer recognise the Paris in which I lived . . . Five years away were enough . . . I feel as though I'm in a foreign city . . ."

He clenched his jaws as if to prevent the words tumbling from his lips in a confused stream. He had probably not spoken to anyone for a long time.

"People no longer reply to telephone calls . . . I don't know whether they're still alive, whether they've forgotten me, or whether they don't have time anymore to take a call . . ."

His grin had grown broader, his expression gentler. Perhaps he meant to cushion the sadness of his words, a sadness that was in keeping with the deserted terrace where the lighting created pools of dim light.

He seemed to regret having confided these matters. He sat

up straight and looked over towards the glazed terrace door. In spite of the coarsening of his face and the grey curls that now made his hair look like a wig, he retained that statuesque stillness that he often displayed ten years ago, one of the rare images of Jacques Perrin de Lara that Daragane remembered. And he also had the habit of frequently turning his head in profile when speaking to people, as he did at this moment. He must have once been told that he had a rather fine profile, but all those who had told him so were dead.

"Do you live in the neighbourhood?" Daragane asked him.

Once again, he leant over towards him and was hesitant in his reply.

"Not very far away . . . in a small hotel in the Ternes district . . ."

"You must give me the address . . ."

"Would you really like me to?"

"Yes . . . I'd be happy to see you again."

He was now going to get to the heart of the matter. And he felt some apprehension. He cleared his throat.

"I'd like to ask you for some information . . ."

His voice was hollow. He noticed the surprise on Perrin de Lara's face.

"It's to do with somebody you may have known . . . Annie Astrand . . ."

He had spoken this name quite loudly and articulated the syllables carefully, as you do on the telephone when interference is likely to muffle your voice.

"Tell me the name again . . ."

"ANNIE ASTRAND."

He had almost yelled it out and he felt as though he had been sending out a call for help.

"I lived at her home for a long time in a house at Saint-Leu-la-Forêt . . ."

The words he had just uttered were very clear and sounded metallic in the silence of this terrace, but he thought they made no difference.

"Yes . . . I see . . . we went to visit you there once, with your mother . . ."

He stopped speaking, and he would say nothing further on the subject. It was purely a distant memory that did not concern him. One should never expect anyone to reply to one's questions.

Nevertheless, he added:

"A very young woman . . . the night-club dancer sort . . . Bob Bugnand and Torstel knew her better than I did . . . and your mother too . . . I believe she had been in prison . . . And so why are you interested in this woman?"

"She meant a great deal to me."

"Ah, really . . . Well, I'm sorry not to be able to give you any information . . . I had vaguely heard of her through your mother and Bob Bugnand . . ."

His voice had taken on a sociable tone. Daragane wondered whether he was not imitating someone who had impressed him in his youth and whose mannerisms and way of speaking he had practised imitating, in the evening in front of a mirror, someone who for him, a decent, slightly naive lad, represented the height of Parisian elegance.

"The only thing that I can tell you is that she had been in prison . . . I really know nothing else about this woman . . ."

The neon lighting on the terrace had been switched off so as to make these last two customers realise that the café was about to close. Perrin de Lara sat there silently in the half-light. Daragane thought of the cinema in Montparnasse that he had gone into the other evening to shelter from the rain. It was not heated and the few people in the audience were still wearing their overcoats. He often kept his eyes closed in the cinema. The voices and the music in a film were more evocative for him than the image. A remark from the film he had seen that evening came to mind, spoken in a muffled voice, before the lights went on, and he had been deceived into thinking that it was he himself who had spoken it: "What a peculiar path I've had to take in order to reach you."

Someone was tapping him on the shoulder:

"Gentlemen, we're about to close . . . It's time to leave . . ."

They had crossed the avenue and were walking through the garden at the spot where, during the daytime, the stalls of the postage stamp market are set up. Daragane hesitated whether to take his leave of Perrin de Lara. The man had stopped suddenly, as though an idea had suddenly crossed his mind:

"I couldn't even tell you why she had been in prison . . ."

He held out a hand which Daragane clasped.

"See you very soon, I hope . . . Or perhaps in ten years' time . . ."

Daragane did not know how to answer him and he stood there, on the pavement, gazing after him. Wearing his far too flimsy coat, the man receded into the distance. He walked beneath the trees very slowly and, at the moment that he was about to cross avenue de Marigny, he almost lost his balance, propelled forward by a puff of wind and an armful of dead leaves.

BACK AT HOME, HE LISTENED TO THE ANSWERING machine to find out whether Chantal Grippay or Gilles Ottolini had left a message. None. The black dress with swallows was still lying on the back of the sofa and the orange cardboard folder was in the same place on his desk, by the telephone. He took out the photocopies.

Not a great deal, at first sight, about Annie Astrand. And yet there was. The address of the house at Saint-Leu-la-Forêt was mentioned: "15 rue de l'Ermitage", followed by a comment that an investigation had taken place there. It had happened in the same year that Annie had taken him to the Photomaton shop and when she had been searched at the customs post at Ventimiglia. Her brother Pierre (6 rue Laferrière, Paris IXe) was mentioned as was Roger Vincent (12 rue Nicolas-Chuquet, Paris XVIIe), whom they wondered might not be her "protector".

It even specified that the house at Saint-Leu-la-Forêt was in the name of Roger Vincent. There were also copies of a much older report from the Criminal Investigation Department, Vice Squad, Investigation and Information Bureau, concerning the aforementioned Astrand Annie living in a hotel, 46 rue Notre-Dame-de-Lorette, on which was written: "Known at the Étoile Kléber". But all this was unclear, as though someone – Ottolini? – when copying out documents from the archives in a hurry, had skipped words and had jumbled together certain sentences taken at random that had no connection one with the other.

Was it really worthwhile burying oneself in this dense and viscous mass again? As he continued with his reading, Daragane experienced a feeling similar to that of the previous day when he tried to decipher the same pages: sentences you hear in a semi-slumber, and the few words you do remember in the morning make no sense. All this, strewn with specific addresses – 15 rue de l'Ermitage, 12 rue Nicolas-Chuquet, 46 rue Notre-Dame-de-Lorette – probably in order to find reference points in this shifting sand.

He was sure that he would tear up these pages over the coming days and that this would make him feel better. Between now and then, he would leave them on his desk. One final reading might conceivably help him discover hidden clues that would put him on the trail of Annie Astrand.

He needed to find the envelope that she had sent him, years ago, containing the passport photos. On the day he received it, he had consulted the current street directory. No Annie Astrand at number 18 rue Alfred-Dehodencq. And since she had not given him her phone number, all he could do was write to her . . . But would he receive an answer from her?

That evening, in his study, all this seemed so long ago . . . It was already ten years since the beginning of the new century . . . And yet, at a bend in the road, or spotting a passing face – and often it only required an unexpected word in a conversation or a note of music – the name, Annie Astrand, came back into his memory. But it happened increasingly seldom and more and more briefly, a bright signal that faded immediately.

He had hesitated whether to write to her or send her a telegram. 18 rue Alfred-Dehodencq. PLEASE GIVE PHONE NUMBER. JEAN. Or a pneumatic dispatch, of the kind that people still sent in those days. And then he, who neither liked unexpected visits nor people who suddenly accost you in the street, had decided to call at that address.

IT WAS IN AUTUMN, ON ALL SAINTS' DAY. IT WAS sunny, that afternoon. For the first time in his life, the words "All Saints" did not instil in him a feeling of sadness. At place Blanche, he had taken the métro. Two changes were required. At Étoile and Trocadéro. On Sundays and public holidays, the trains took a long time coming, and he thought to himself that he would have been unable to have seen Annie Astrand again except on a public holiday. He counted the years: fifteen, since the afternoon she had taken him to the Photomaton shop. He remembered a morning, at the gare de Lyon. They had both boarded the train, a crowded train on the first day of the summer holidays.

While waiting for the train at Trocadéro station, he had a sudden doubt: she might not be in Paris that day. After fifteen years, he would no longer recognise her.

There were railings at the end of the street. Behind them

were the trees in the Ranelagh gardens. Not a single car the entire length of the pavement. The silence. Hard to imagine anyone living here. Number 18 was at the very end, on the right, before the railings and the trees. A white building, or rather a large house with two storeys. At the entrance door, an intercom. And a name, alongside the single button of this intercom: VINCENT.

The building seemed to him to be deserted, like the street. He pressed the button. From the intercom, he heard a crackling sound, which could have been the rustle of the wind in the trees. He leant forward and, enunciating the syllables clearly, he said twice: "JEAN DARAGANE". A woman's voice, partly muffled by the noise of the wind, replied: "First floor."

The glazed door opened slowly and he found himself in a white entrance hall lit by a wall lamp. He did not take the lift and went up by the right-angled staircase. When he reached the landing, she was standing at the half-open door, her face partly hidden. Then she drew back the door and stared at him as though she had difficulty recognising him.

"Come in, Jean dear . . ."

A timid, but slightly husky voice, just as it had been fifteen years ago. The face had not altered either, nor had the expression. Her hair was not as short. It reached down to her shoulders. How old was she now? Thirty-six? In the hallway, she was still looking at him with curiosity. He tried to think of something to say to her:

"I didn't know whether I should press the button that said 'Vincent'..."

"My name is Vincent now ... I've even changed my first name, would you believe ... Agnès Vincent..."

She showed him into the adjoining room, which was probably used as a drawing room, although the only furniture consisted of a sofa and, next to it, a floor lamp. A large bay window through which he could see trees that had not lost their leaves. It was still light. Glimmers of sunshine on the wooden floor and on the walls.

"Sit down, Jean dear..."

She sat down at the other end of the sofa, as if to observe him better.

"Do you remember Roger Vincent, perhaps?"

Scarcely had she uttered this name than he did in fact remember an American car, a convertible, parked outside the house at Saint-Leu-la-Forêt, and in the driver's seat sat a man, whom he had assumed, at first, was also American on account of his height and a slight accent when he spoke.

"I got married a few years ago to Roger Vincent..."

She looked at him and she had an embarrassed smile on

her face. So that he should forgive her for this marriage?

"He's in Paris less and less . . . I think he'd be glad to see you again . . . I phoned him the other day and I told him that you had written a book . . ."

One afternoon, at Saint-Leu-la-Forêt, Roger Vincent had come to collect him outside school in his convertible American car. It glided so quietly along rue de l'Ermitage that you could not hear the sound of the engine.

"I haven't read your book to the end yet . . . I stumbled on the passage about the Photomaton shop straight away . . . I never read novels, you know . . ."

She seemed to be apologising, as she had done just now when she had informed him about her marriage to Roger Vincent. But no, there was no point in her reading the book "to the end" now that they were sitting on the sofa together.

"You must have wondered how I was able to get your address . . . I met someone who drove you home last year . . ."

She frowned and seemed to be searching for a name. But Daragane himself came up with:

"Guy Torstel?"

"Yes . . . Guy Torstel . . ."

Why do people whose existence you are unaware of, whom you meet once and will never see again, come to play, behind the scenes, an important role in your life? Thanks to this individual, he had found Annie again. He would have liked to thank this Torstel.

"I'd completely forgotten this man . . . He must live in the neighbourhood . . . He accosted me in the street . . . He told me that he had come to the house at Saint-Leu-la-Forêt fifteen years ago . . ."

It was probably this meeting with Torstel at the racecourse last autumn that had jogged his memory of her. Torstel had talked about the house at Saint-Leu-la-Forêt. When Torstel had said: "I can't remember what this place on the outskirts of Paris was", and also: "The child, it was you, I imagine", he, Daragane, had not wished to answer. He had not thought about Annie Astrand, or about Saint-Leu-la-Forêt for a long time. However, this encounter had suddenly revived memories that, without his being fully aware of them, he was careful not to awaken. And now, he had done so. They were very tenacious, these memories. That very evening he began to write his book.

"He told me that he had met you at a racecourse . . ."

She smiled as though it were a joke.

"I hope you're not a gambler."

"No, not at all."

He, a gambler? He had never understood why all these people in casinos spent so long standing around tables, silent and motionless, looking as though they were more dead than alive. And every time Paul had talked to him about doubling up on his losses, he found it difficult to maintain his concentration.

"With gamblers, things always end up very badly, Jean dear."

Perhaps she knew a great deal about the subject. She frequently used to return very late to the house at Saint-Leu-la-Forêt, and he, Daragane, had sometimes found he could not get to sleep until she returned. What a comfort to hear the sound of her car's tyres on the gravel and the engine which you knew was about to be switched off. And her footsteps along the corridor . . . What did she do in Paris until two in the morning? Perhaps she gambled. After all these years, and now that he was no longer a child, he would have liked to put the question to her.

"I didn't really understand what this Monsieur Torstel does . . . I believe he's an antique dealer at the Palais-Royal . . ."

It was clear she did not know what to say to him. He would have liked to make her feel at ease. She probably felt as he did, as though there were a shadowy presence between them, which neither of them was able to speak about.

"So, you're a writer now?"

She was smiling at him, and this smile struck him as

ironical. A writer. Why not confess to her that he had written *Le Noir de l'été* in the style of a missing person advertisement? With a bit of luck, the book would attract her attention, and she would get in touch with him. That is what he had thought. Nothing more.

The daylight was fading, but she did not switch on the standard lamp beside her.

"I should have got in touch with you before now, but I had rather a turbulent life . . ."

She had just used the perfect tense, as though her life were over.

"It didn't surprise me that you should have become a writer. When you were little, at Saint-Leu-la-Forêt, you read a lot..."

Daragane would have preferred her to talk about her own life, but she seemed not to want to do so. She was sitting on the sofa, in profile. An image that had retained great clarity, in spite of all these lost years, came back to him. One afternoon, Annie, in the same position, head and shoulders to the right, in profile, seated at the wheel of her car and he, a child, beside her. The car was parked outside the gate of the house, at Saint-Leu-la-Forêt. He had noticed a tear, barely visible, slipping down her right cheek. She had made a sudden movement with her elbow to wipe it away. Then she started up the engine, as though nothing were the matter.

"Last year," said Daragane, "I met someone else who knew you . . . in the Saint-Leu-la Forêt days . . ."

She turned towards him and cast him an anxious look. "Who?"

"A Jacques Perrin de Lara."

"No, I can't think who . . . I met so many people in the Saint-Leu-la-Forêt days . . ."

"And Bob Bugnand, does that mean anything to you?"

"No, nothing at all."

She had drawn closer to him and was stroking his forehead.

"What's going on inside that head of yours, Jean dear? Do you want to cross-question me?"

She looked him full in the eyes. No threat in this gaze. Just a slight anxiety. She stroked his forehead again.

"You know . . . I've got a bad memory . . ."

He recalled Perrin de Lara's words: "The only thing I can tell you is that she had been in prison." If he were to repeat this to her, she would show huge surprise. She would shrug and she would reply to him, "He must be confusing me with someone else", or else, "And you believed him, Jean dear?" And perhaps she would be genuine. In the end, we forget the details of our lives that embarrass us or are too painful. We just lie back and allow ourselves to float along calmly over the deep waters, with our eyes closed. No, it is not always a matter of deliberate forgetfulness, a doctor whom he had engaged in conversation had explained to him, in the café below the blocks of flats in square du Graisivaudan. This man had also inscribed a little book to him that he had written for Presses universitaires de France, *L'Oubli*.

"Do you want me to explain why I took you to have passport photos made?"

Daragane felt she was not embarking on this subject willingly. But dusk was closing in and, in this drawing room, the dim light could make revelations easier.

"It's very simple . . . In the absence of your parents, I wanted to take you with me to Italy . . . but for that, you needed a passport . . ."

In the yellow cardboard suitcase that he had humped around from room to room for some years, which contained exercise books, certificates, postcards sent to him when he was a child and the books that he was reading at that time – *Arbre, mon ami*, *Le Cargo du mystère*, *Le Cheval sans tête*, *Les Mille et Une Nuits* – there might be an old passport in his name, with the photograph, one of those navy-blue passports. But he never opened the suitcase. It was locked, and he had lost the key. Like the passport, no doubt.

"And then, I wasn't able to take you to Italy . . . I had to stay in France . . . We spent a few days on the Côte d'Azur . . . And afterwards, you went back home . . ."

His father had come to collect him from an empty house, and they had caught the train back to Paris. What exactly had she meant by "home"? However much he racked his memory, he had not the slightest recollection of what in present-day language is known as "a home of one's own". The train had arrived, very early in the morning at the gare de Lyon. And after that, long, endless years of boarding school.

"When I read the passage in your book, I searched among my papers and I found the passport photos . . ."

Daragane would have to wait for over forty years to learn another detail of this affair: the passport photos of an "un-identified child" that had been confiscated during a search at the customs post at Ventimiglia. "All I know about this woman," Perrin de Lara had said to him, "is that she had been in prison." In that case, the passport photographs and other things removed during the search when she was re-leased from prison had certainly been returned to her. But sitting beside her there, on this sofa, Daragane did not yet know these details. We discover, often too late to talk to them about it, an episode from their life that a loved one has concealed from you. Has he really hidden it from you? He has forgotten, or more likely, over time, he no longer thinks about it. Or, quite simply, he can't find the words.

"It's a pity we weren't able to go to Italy," said Daragane with a big smile.

He sensed that she wanted to tell him something in confidence. But she shook her head gently, as though she were dismissing bad thoughts – or bad memories.

"So, you live in square du Graisivaudan?"

"Not really anymore. I found a room to let in another neighbourhood."

The owner was not in Paris and so he had kept the key to the square du Graisivaudan room. So, he did go there illegally sometimes. The prospect of taking refuge in two different places put his mind at ease.

"Yes, a room near place Blanche . . ."

"At Blanche?"

This word seemed to conjure up a terrain that was familiar to her.

"Will you take me to your room one day?"

It was almost dark, and she switched on the standard lamp. They were both sitting in the middle of a halo of light, and the drawing room remained in the shade.

"I knew the place Blanche area well . . . Do you remember my brother Pierre? He had a garage over there."

A young man with dark hair. At Saint-Leu-la-Forêt, he

sometimes slept in the small bedroom, on the left, at the end of the corridor, the one with the window that gave onto the courtyard and the well. Daragane remembered his sheepskin jacket and his car, a Renault 4. One Sunday, this brother of Annie's – after all this time, he had forgotten his first name – had taken him to the Cirque Médrano. Afterwards, they had driven back in the Renault 4 to Saint-Leu-la-Forêt.

"I haven't seen Pierre since I've been living here . . ."

"Strange sort of place," said Daragane.

And he looked around at the bay window – a large black screen behind which the leaves of the trees could no longer be seen.

"We're in the back of beyond here, Jean dear. Don't you think?"

He had been surprised earlier by the silence of the street and by the railings that created a dead end to the road. When night fell, you could imagine the building being on the edge of a forest.

"It's Roger Vincent who's rented this house since the war . . . It had been impounded . . . It belonged to people who must have left France . . . With Roger Vincent, you know, things are always a bit complicated . . ."

She called him "Roger Vincent", and never simply "Roger". Daragane, too, as a child, used to greet him with a "Good morning, Roger Vincent".

"I'm not going to be able to stay here . . . They're going to let the house to an embassy, or knock it down . . . At night, sometimes, I'm frightened of finding myself all alone here . . . The ground floor and the second floor are unoccupied . . . And Roger Vincent is hardly ever there."

She preferred to talk to him about the present, and Daragane understood this very well. He wondered whether this woman was the same person whom he had known, as a child, at Saint-Leu-la-Forêt. And as for himself, who was he? Forty years later, when the enlargement of the passport photograph would fall into his hands, he would no longer even know whether that child was himself.

Later on, she had wanted to take him to have dinner, close to where she lived, and they had ended up in a brasserie on Chaussée de la Muette. They were sitting, opposite one another, at the very back of the restaurant.

"I remember that we sometimes used to go together to the restaurant, at Saint-Leu-la-Forêt," Daragane said to her.

"Are you sure?"

"The restaurant was called Chalet de l'Ermitage."

This name had struck him as a child because it was the same as that of the street.

She shrugged.

"I'm amazed . . . I would never have taken a child to a restaurant . . ."

She had said this in a stern voice that surprised Daragane.

"Did you stay much longer in the house at Saint-Leu-la-Forêt?"

"No . . . Roger Vincent sold it . . . That house belonged to Roger Vincent, you know."

He had always believed that it was Annie Astrand's house. At the time, these two names seemed to him to be linked: Anniastrand.

"I spent about a year there, didn't I?"

He had asked the question that was on the tip of his tongue, as though he were afraid it might not be answered.

"Yes . . . one year . . . I'm not sure . . . your mother wanted you to have some country air . . . I had the impression that she was trying to get rid of you . . ."

"How did you come to know her?"

"Oh . . . through friends . . . I used to meet so many people in those days . . ."

Daragane realised that she was not going to tell him much about that time at Saint-Leu-la-Forêt. He would have to be satisfied with his own memories, memories that were sparse and few and which he was no longer even sure were accurate, since she had just told him that she would never have taken a child to a restaurant.

"Forgive me, Jean dear . . . I hardly ever think of the past . . ."

She paused for a moment, and then:

"I had some difficulties at the time . . . I don't know whether you remember Colette?"

This name awoke a very vague recollection in him, as elusive as a reflection that flickers all too briefly on a wall.

"Colette . . . Colette Laurent . . . There was a portrait of her in my bedroom, at Saint-Leu-la-Forêt . . . she used to pose for artists . . . She was a friend from teenage days . . ."

He clearly remembered the painting between the two windows. A girl with her elbows on a table, her chin in the palm of her hand.

"She was murdered in a hotel in Paris . . . no-one ever knew who by . . . She often used to come to Saint-Leu-la-Forêt . . ."

When Annie returned from Paris, at about two o'clock in the morning, he had heard shrieks of laughter in the corridor on several occasions. That meant she was not alone. Then the bedroom door was closed and mutterings would reach him through the partitions. One morning, they had given this Colette Laurent a lift to Paris in Annie's car. She was sitting in the front, beside Annie, and he was alone on the back seat.

They had walked with her in the Champs-Élysées gardens, where the postage stamp market was situated. They had stopped at one of the stalls, and Colette Laurent had given him a pack of stamps, a series of different colours bearing the image of the king of Egypt. From that day on, he had begun to collect stamps. The album in which he arranged them gradually in rows behind strips of transparent paper, this album may have been put away in the cardboard suitcase. He had not opened that suitcase for ten years. He could not part with it, but he was nevertheless relieved to have lost the key.

On another day, they had gone, with Colette Laurent, to a village on the other side of Montmorency forest. Annie had parked her car outside a sort of small château, and she had explained to him that this was the boarding school where she and Colette Laurent had met. They had visited the boarding school with him, shown round by the headmistress. The classrooms and the dormitories were deserted.

"So, you don't remember Colette?"

"Yes . . . of course," said Daragane. "You knew each other at boarding school."

She looked at him in surprise.

"How did you know?"

"One afternoon, you took me to visit your old boarding school."

"Are you sure? I have no memory of it."

"It was on the other side of Montmorency forest."

"I never took you there with Colette . . ."

He did not want to contradict her. He might find explanations in the book that the doctor had inscribed to him, that little book with white covers about forgetfulness.

They were walking along the footpath, next to the Ranelagh gardens. Because of the night, the trees and the presence of Annie, who had taken his arm, Daragane had the impression that he was walking with her, as he used to do, in the Montmorency forest. She stopped the car at a crossroads in the forest, and they walked as far as the Fossombrone pond. He remembered some of the names: the Chêne aux Mouches crossroads. The La Pointe crossroads. One of these names made him feel frightened: the Prince de Condé's cross. At the little school at which Annie had enrolled him and from which she often came to collect him at half-past four, the teacher had talked about this prince whom they had discovered hanged in his bedroom at the château of Saint-Leu without anyone ever knowing the precise circumstances of his death. She called him "the last of the Condés".

"What are you thinking about, Jean dear?"

She was leaning her head on his shoulder, and Daragane

wanted to tell her that he was thinking about "the last of the Condés", about school and about walks in the forest. But he was afraid she might reply: "No . . . You're wrong . . . I haven't any memory of it." He, too, during these past fifteen years, had eventually forgotten everything.

"You must invite me to your room . . . I should like to go back to the place Blanche neighbourhood with you."

Perhaps she remembered that they had spent a few days in this neighbourhood before leaving by train for the south of France. But, there again, he did not dare put the question to her.

"You would find the room too small . . ." said Daragane. "And besides, it's not heated . . ."

"That doesn't matter . . . you can't imagine how we used to freeze to death in this neighbourhood, in winter, when we were very young, my brother Pierre and I."

And at least this memory was not painful to her, since she burst out laughing.

They had reached the end of the footpath, very close to the Porte de la Muette. He wondered whether this smell of autumn, of leaves and moist earth, did not come from the Bois de Boulogne. Or else, over time, from the Montmorency forest.

*

They had made a detour to rejoin what she called, with a touch of irony, her "place of residence". As they walked along together, he felt himself overcome by a gentle amnesia. Eventually, he came to wonder how long he had been in the company of this stranger. Perhaps he had just met her, on the path by the gardens or outside one of these buildings without any windows at the front. And if he happened to notice a light, it was always at the window of a floor at the very top, as though somebody had left a long time ago and forgotten to switch off a lamp.

She squeezed his arm, and it was though she wanted to reassure herself of his presence.

"I always feel frightened when I come back home on foot, at this sort of time . . . I no longer know exactly where I am . . ."

And it was true that they were crossing a no-man's-land, or rather a neutral zone in which they were cut off from everything.

"Supposing you needed to buy a pack of cigarettes or find a chemist open at night . . . it's very difficult around here . . ."

Once again, she burst out laughing. Her laughter and the noise of their footsteps echoed in these streets, one of which bore the name of a forgotten writer.

She took a bunch of keys out of her coat pocket and tried

several of them in the front door lock before finding the right one.

"Jean . . . will you come up with me . . . ? I'm frightened of ghosts . . ."

They were in the hallway with its black and white tiling. She opened a double door.

"Would you like me to show you round the ground floor?"

A suite of empty rooms. Pale wooden floors and large bay windows. A white light beamed down from the built-in wall lamps, just below the ceiling.

"This must have been the drawing room, the dining room and the library . . . At one time, Roger Vincent used to store goods here . . ."

She closed the door, took his arm and led him towards the staircase.

"Would you like to see the second floor?"

Once again, she opened a door and switched on the light which came from the same kind of wall lamps at ceiling-height. An empty room like those on the ground floor. She slid back one of the bay windows, in which the glass was cracked. A large balcony overlooked the trees in the gardens.

"It was the former owner's gym room . . . The one who lived here before the war . . ."

Daragane noticed some holes in the floor, a floor that appeared to have the consistency of cork. Attached to the wall was a piece of wooden furniture with slots that supported some small dumbbells.

"It's full of ghosts here . . . I never come here just on my own."

On the first floor, by the door, she put a hand on his shoulder.

"Jean . . . Can you stay with me tonight?"

She led him into the room that was used as a drawing room. She did not switch on the light. On the sofa, she leant over and whispered in his ear:

"When I have to leave here, will you put me up at your room in place Blanche?"

She stroked his forehead. And, still in a low voice:

"Pretend that we hadn't known each other before. It's easy . . ."

Yes, it was easy after all, since she had told him that she had changed her name, and even her first name.

AT ABOUT ELEVEN O'CLOCK AT NIGHT, THE TELEPHONE rang in his study, but he did not pick up the receiver and waited for a message to be left on the answering machine. Breathing, regular at first, then increasingly halting, and a faraway voice; he wondered whether it was a woman's or a man's. A groan. Then the breathing began again and two voices mingled with one another and whispered without his being able to distinguish the words. Eventually, he turned off the answering machine and disconnected the telephone. Who was it? Chantal Grippay? Gilles Ottolini? Both of them at the same time?

In the end, he decided to take advantage of the silence of the night to reread all the pages of the "dossier" for one last time. But no sooner had he started his reading than he experienced an unpleasant sensation: the sentences became muddled and other sentences suddenly appeared that overlaid the previous ones and disappeared without giving him time to decipher them. He was confronted with a palimpsest in which all the various writings were jumbled together and superimposed, and moved about like bacilli seen through a microscope. He put this down to weariness, and he closed his eyes.

When he opened them again, he came across the photocopy of the passage in *Le Noir de l'été* in which the name of Guy Torstel was mentioned. Apart from the episode of the Photomaton shop – an episode he had stolen from real life – he had not the slightest memory of his first book. The only one he retained was that of the first twenty pages which he had later suppressed. In his mind's eye, they were to have been the beginning of the book before he abandoned it. He had visualised a title for this first chapter: "Return to Saint-Leu-la-Forêt". Were these twenty pages still hibernating in a cardboard box or an old suitcase? Or had he torn them up? He no longer knew.

Before writing them, he had wanted to travel for one last time, after fifteen years, to Saint-Leu-la-Forêt. It was not so much a pilgrimage, but rather a visit that would help him write the beginning of the book. And he had not mentioned this "return to Saint-Leu-la-Forêt" to Annie Astrand a few months later, on the evening he had seen her again after the book had been published. He was frightened that she might shrug and say to him: "But what a strange idea, Jean dear, to go back there . . ."

So, one afternoon, a few days after having met Torstel at the racecourse, he had taken a bus to Porte d'Asnières. The suburb had already changed a good deal at that time. Was it the same route that Annie Astrand had taken when she came back by car from Paris? The bus passed under the railway track near Ermont station. And yet he now wondered whether he had not dreamt this journey, which had taken place over forty years ago. It was probably the fact that he had made it a chapter of his novel that induced such confusion in him. He had walked up Saint-Leu's main street and crossed the square with the fountain . . . A yellow mist hovered and he wondered whether it did not come from the forest. On rue de l'Ermitage, he was sure that the majority of the houses had not yet been built in Annie Astrand's time and that in their place there had been trees, on either side, the canopies of which formed an archway. Was he really in Saint-Leu? He thought he recognised the part of the house that gave onto the street and the large porch beneath which Annie often parked her car. But, further along, the surrounding wall had vanished and a long, concrete building replaced it.

Opposite, protected by a metal gate, was a single-storey house with a bow window and a frontage covered in ivy. A copper plate on the gate: "DR LOUIS VOUSTRAAT". He remembered that after school one morning Annie had taken him to this doctor, and that one evening the doctor himself had come to the house to see him in his bedroom because he was ill.

He hesitated for a moment, there, in the middle of the street, then he made up his mind. He pushed open the gate which gave onto a small garden and he walked up the stone steps. He rang the bell, and waited. Through the half-open door, he saw a tall man, his white hair cut short, with blue eyes. He did not recognise him.

"Doctor Voustraat?"

The man gave a start of surprise, as though Daragane had just roused him from his slumber.

"There is no surgery today."

"I merely wanted to talk to you."

"What about, monsieur?"

Nothing suspicious about this question. His tone was friendly and there was something reassuring about his voice.

"I'm writing a book about Saint-Leu-la-Forêt . . . I wanted to ask you a few questions."

Daragane felt so nervous that he thought he might have spoken this sentence with a stutter. The man gazed at him with a smile.

"Come in, monsieur."

He led him into a drawing room where a fire was burning in the grate and directed him to an armchair opposite the bow window. He sat down beside him in a similar armchair that was covered in the same tartan material.

"And who gave you the notion of coming to see me, in particular?"

His voice was so solemn and gentle that, within a very short time, he could have extracted confessions from the wiliest and most hardened criminal. At least that was what Daragane imagined.

"Passing by, I saw your plate. And I said to myself that a doctor knows the place where he practises very well . . ."

He had tried to speak clearly, in spite of his awkwardness, and he had only just managed to use the word "place" instead of "village", which was the one that had automatically come to mind. But Saint-Leu-la-Forêt was no longer the village of his childhood.

"You are not mistaken. I've been practising here for twenty-five years."

He stood up and walked over to a shelf on which Daragane noticed a box of liqueurs.

"Will you drink something? A little port?"

He handed the glass to Daragane and sat down again, beside him, in the tartan-covered armchair.

"And you are writing a book about Saint-Leu? What a good idea . . ."

"Oh . . . a pamphlet . . . for a series on the different areas of Île-de-France . . ."

He searched for other details that would inspire this Dr Voustraat with confidence.

"For example, I'm devoting a chapter to the mysterious death of the last Prince de Condé."

"I can see that you are well acquainted with the history of our little town."

And Dr Voustraat stared at him with his blue eyes and smiled at him, as he had done fifteen years ago when he had listened to his chest in his bedroom in the house opposite. Was it for a bout of flu or for one of those childhood illnesses with such complicated names?

"I shall need other information that may not be historical," said Daragane. "Some anecdotes, for example, concerning certain inhabitants of the town . . ."

He astonished himself at having been able to complete a sentence of such length, and with confidence.

Dr Voustraat appeared thoughtful, his eyes focused on a log that was burning gently in the grate.

"We have had artists at Saint-Leu," he said as he nodded, looking as though he were jogging his memory. "The pianist

Wanda Landowska . . . And also the poet Olivier Larronde . . ."

"Would you mind if I made a note of the names?" Daragane asked.

From one of his coat pockets he took out a ballpoint pen and the black moleskin notebook that he always kept with him since he had begun his book. In it, he jotted down snatches of sentences, or possible titles for his novel. With great care, he wrote, in capital letters: WANDA LANDOWSKA. OLIVIER LARRONDE. He wanted to show Dr Voustraat that he had scholarly habits.

"Thank you for your information."

"Other names will certainly occur to me . . ."

"It's very kind of you," said Daragane. "Would you, by any chance, remember a news item that is supposed to have occured at Saint-Leu-la-Forêt?"

"A news item?"

Dr Voustraat was evidently surprised by this word.

"Not a crime, of course . . . But something shady that may have happened around here . . . I was told about a house, just opposite yours, where some strange people lived . . ."

There, he had cut to the heart of the matter, in a much quicker way than he had anticipated.

Dr Voustraat's blue eyes stared at him again and Daragane sensed a certain mistrust in his gaze.

"Which house opposite?"

He wondered whether he had not gone too far. But why, after all? Did he not appear to be a sensible young man who wanted to write a pamphlet about Saint-Leu-la-Forêt?

"The house that's slightly to the right . . . with the large porch . . ."

"You mean La Maladrerie?"

Daragane had forgotten this name, which caused him a pang of emotion. He had the fleeting sense of passing beneath the porch of the house.

"Yes, that's it . . . La Maladrerie . . ." and pronouncing these five syllables he suddenly experienced a feeling of dizziness, or rather of fear, as though La Maladrerie were associated for him with a bad dream.

"Who spoke to you about La Maladrerie?"

He was taken aback. It would have been better to tell Dr Voustraat the truth. Now, it was too late. He should have done so earlier, on the doorstep. "You looked after me, a very long time ago, during my childhood." But no, he would have felt like an imposter and as though he were stealing someone else's identity. That child seemed like a stranger to him now.

"It was the owner of the Ermitage restaurant who spoke to me about it . . ."

He said this just in case, to put him off the track. Did this establishment still exist, and had it ever really existed apart from in his memories?

"Ah, yes . . . the Ermitage restaurant. I didn't think it was called that anymore, nowadays . . . Have you known Saint-Leu for a long time?"

Daragane sensed a surge of dizziness welling up inside him, the kind that affects you when you are on the brink of confessing to something that will alter the course of your life. There, at the top of the slope, you just have to let yourself glide, as though on a slide. At the bottom of the large garden at La Maladrerie, there had actually been a slide, probably erected by the previous owners, and its handrail was rusty.

"No. It's the first time I've been to Saint-Leu-la-Forêt."

Outside, dusk was falling, and Dr Voustraat stood up to switch on a lamp and stoke the fire.

"Wintry weather . . . Did you see that fog just now? . . . I was right to make a fire . . ."

He sat down in the armchair and leant over towards Daragane.

"You were lucky to have rung my bell today . . . It's my day off . . . I should also mention that I've cut down on the number of my home visits . . ."

Was this word "visits" a hint on his part that implied he had recognised him? But there had been so many home visits over the last fifteen years and so many appointments at Dr Louis Voustraat's home, in the little room that served as his surgery, at the end of the corridor, that he could not recognise all the faces. And in any case, thought Daragane, how could one ascertain a likeness between that child and the person he was today?

"La Maladrerie was indeed lived in by some strange people . . . But do you think there's really any point in my talking to you about them?"

Daragane had the sense that there was something more behind these harmless words. As on the radio, for example, when the sound is blurred and two voices are broadcast one over the other. He seemed to be hearing: "Why have you come back to Saint-Leu after fifteen years?"

"It's as though this house had a curse put on it . . . Perhaps because of its name . . ."

"Its name?"

Dr Voustraat smiled at him.

"Do you know what 'maladrerie' means?"

"Of course," said Daragane.

He did not know, but he was ashamed to admit this to Dr Voustraat.

"Before the war, it was lived in by a doctor like me who left Saint-Leu . . . Later on, at the time I arrived, a certain Lucien

Führer used to come here regularly . . . the owner of a sleazy Paris dive . . . There were many comings and goings . . . It was from this time on that the house was visited by some strange people . . . up until the end of the fifties . . ."

Daragane jotted down the doctor's words in his notebook as he went along. It was as though he were about to reveal the secret of his origins to him, all those years from the beginning of one's life that had been forgotten, apart from the occasional detail that rises up from the depths, a street entirely covered by a canopy of leaves, a smell, a name that is familiar but which you no longer know whom it belonged to, a slide.

"And then this Lucien Führer disappeared from one day to the next, and the house was bought by a Monsieur Vincent . . . Roger Vincent, if I remember correctly . . . He always parked his American convertible in the street . . ."

After fifteen years, Daragane was not entirely sure what colour this car was. Beige? Yes, surely. With red leather seats. Dr Voustraat remembered that it was a convertible and, if he had a good memory, he might have been able to confirm this colour: beige. But he feared that if he asked him this question, he might arouse his suspicion.

"I could not tell you exactly what this Monsieur Roger Vincent's job was . . . perhaps the same as Lucien Führer's . . . A man of about forty who came from Paris frequently . . ."

It seemed to Daragane in those days that Roger Vincent never slept at the house. He would spend the day at Saint-Leu-la-Forêt and leave again after dinner. From his bed, he could hear him starting up his car, and the noise was different from Annie's car. A noise both louder and more muffled.

"People said that he was half American or that he'd spent a long time in America . . . He had the look of an American . . . Tall . . . sporty in his appearance . . . I treated him once . . . I believe he had dislocated his wrist . . ."

Daragane had no memory of that. He would have been impressed if he had seen Roger Vincent wearing a bandage on his wrist or a plaster.

"There was also a young woman and a little boy who lived there . . . She wasn't old enough to have been his mother . . . I used to think that she was his big sister . . . She could have been this Monsieur Roger Vincent's daughter . . ."

Roger Vincent's daughter? No, this notion had not occurred to him. He had never asked himself questions as to the precise relationship between Roger Vincent and Annie. It would appear, he often used to say to himself, that children never ask themselves any questions. Many years afterwards, we attempt to solve puzzles that were not mysteries at the time and we try to decipher half-obliterated letters from a language that is too old and whose alphabet we don't even know.

"There were many comings and goings in this house . . . Sometimes, people would arrive in the middle of the night . . ."

In those days, Daragane slept well – the sleep of childhood – except on the evenings when he waited for Annie to return. He would often hear noisy voices and doors banging in the night, but he fell asleep again immediately. And anyway, the house was enormous, a building made up of several different parts, and so he never knew who was there. Leaving to go to school in the morning, he used to notice a number of cars parked in front of the porch. In the part of the building where his bedroom was, there was also Annie's, on the other side of the corridor.

"And, in your opinion, who were all these people?" he asked Dr Voustraat.

"A house search was conducted, but they had all disappeared . . . They questioned me, since I was their nearest neighbour . . . Apparently, this Roger Vincent had been implicated in an affair they called 'The Combination' . . . I must have read this name somewhere, but I couldn't tell you what it's to do with . . . I confess I've never been interested in news items."

Did Daragane really want to know any more than Dr Voustraat did? A gleam of light that you can barely make out from beneath a closed door and which indicates someone is there. But he did not want to open the door in order to discover who was in the room, or rather in the cupboard. A turn of phrase immediately came to mind: "the skeleton in the cupboard". No, he did not want to know what the word "combination" stood for. Ever since childhood, he used to have the same bad dream: huge relief initially, when he woke up, as though he had escaped from a danger. And then, the bad dream became more and more specific. He had been an accomplice or a witness to something serious that had happened very long ago in the past. Certain people had been arrested. He himself had never been identified. He lived under the threat of being interrogated, when they would notice that he had had connections with the "culprits". And it would be impossible for him to answer questions.

"And the young woman with the child?" he said to Dr Voustraat.

He had been surprised when the doctor had said: "I thought she was his big sister." A horizon might be opening up on his life and would dispel the shadowy areas: fickle parents whom he scarcely remembered and who apparently wished to get rid of him. And that house at Saint-Leu-la-Forêt . . . He sometimes wondered what he was doing there. From tomorrow onwards, he would devote himself to making enquiries. And first of all, find Annie Astrand's birth certificate. And also ask for his own, Daragane's, birth certificate, but he would not be satisfied with a typewritten duplicate and he would consult the register, where everything is written in hand, himself. On the few lines devoted to his birth, he would discover crossings-out, alterations, names that they had tried to rub out.

"She was often on her own with the little boy, at La Maladrerie . . . I was asked questions about her as well, after the search . . . According to the people who interrogated me, she had been an 'acrobatic dancer' . . ."

He had pronounced the two last words on the tip of his tongue.

"It's the first time I've spoken to anyone about this business for a long time . . . Apart from me, no-one really knew about it at Saint-Leu . . . I was their nearest neighbour . . . But you must understand that they weren't exactly my kind of people . . ."

He smiled at Daragane, a slightly ironic smile, and Daragane smiled too at the thought that this man with close-cropped white hair, a military bearing, and, especially, his very open blue eyes, had been – as he said – their nearest neighbour.

"I don't think you're going to use all that for your pamphlet about Saint-Leu . . . or else you would have to search for more precise details in the police archives . . . But, in all honesty, do you think that would be worthwhile?"

This question surprised Daragane. Had Dr Voustraat recognised him and seen through him? "In all honesty, do you think that would be worthwhile?" He had said this with kindness, in a tone of fatherly reproach or even friendly advice – the advice of someone who might have known you in your childhood.

"No, of course," said Daragane. "It would be out of place in a simple pamphlet about Saint-Leu-la-Forêt. One could conceivably write a novel about it."

He had set foot on a slippery slope which he was on the point of sliding down: admitting to Doctor Voustraat the precise reasons why he had rung his doorbell. He could even say to him: "Doctor, let's go to your surgery for a consultation, as we used to do in the old days . . . Is it still at the end of the corridor?"

"A novel? You would have to know all the principal characters. Many people have been to this house . . . Those who questioned me used to refer to a list and mentioned every name to me . . . But I didn't know any of those individuals . . ."

Daragane would have really liked to have this list in his possession. It would probably have helped him pick up Annie's trail, but all these people had vanished into thin air, changing their surnames, their first names and their features. Annie herself, if she were still alive, would be unlikely still to be known as Annie.

"And the child?" asked Daragane. "Did you hear any news of the child?"

"None. I've often wondered what became of him . . . What a strange start to life . . ."

"They must surely have registered him at a school . . ."

"Yes. At the Forêt school on rue de Beuvron. I remember having written a note to explain his absence because of flu."

"Perhaps at the Forêt school, we might find some record of his being there . . ."

"No, unfortunately. They pulled down the Forêt school two years ago. It was a very small school, you know . . ."

Daragane remembered the playground, its asphalt surface, its plane trees, and the contrast, on sunny afternoons, between the green of the foliage and the black of the asphalt. And he did not need to close his eyes to do so.

"The school no longer exists, but I can show you around the house . . ."

Once again, he had the feeling that Dr Voustraat had seen through him. But no, that was impossible. There was no longer anything in common between himself and this child he had left behind along with the others, with Annie, Roger Vincent and the people who came at night, by car, and whose names once featured on a list – that of passengers on a sunken ship.

"I was entrusted with a duplicate key to the house . . . in case any of my patients wanted to visit it . . . It's for sale . . . But not many customers have turned up. Shall I take you round?"

"Another time."

Dr Voustraat seemed disappointed. In actual fact, thought Daragane, he was glad to invite me in and to chat. Normally, during these endless afternoons with time to spare, he must be on his own.

"Really? Wouldn't you like to? It's one of the oldest houses in Saint-Leu . . . As its name indicates, it was built on the site of a former lazaretto . . . That could be of interest for your pamphlet . . ."

"Another day," said Daragane. "I promise you I'll be back."

He lacked the courage to go into the house. He preferred that it should remain for him one of those places that have been familiar to you and which you occasionally happen to visit in dreams: in appearance they are the same, and yet they are permeated with something strange. A veil or a light that is too harsh? And in these dreams you come across people you once loved and whom you know are dead. If you speak to them they don't hear your voice.

"Is the furniture still the same as fifteen years ago?"

"There is no longer any furniture," said Dr Voustraat. "All the rooms are empty. And the garden is an absolute virgin forest."

Annie's bedroom, on the other side of the corridor, from where in his semi-slumber he used to hear voices and shrieks of laughter very late into the night. She was accompanied by

Colette Laurent. But, often, the voice and the laugh were those of a man whom he had never met in the house during the daytime. This man must have left very early in the morning, long before school. Someone who would remain a stranger until the end of time. Another more detailed memory came back to him, but effortlessly so, like the words of songs learnt in your childhood and that you are able to recite all your life without understanding them. Her two bedroom windows gave onto the street which was not the same as it is today, a street shaded by trees. On the white wall, opposite her bed, a coloured engraving depicted flowers, fruit and leaves, and underneath it was written in large letters: BELLADONNA AND HENBANE. Much later, he discovered that these were poisonous plants, but at the time what interested him was deciphering the letters: belladonna and henbane, the first words he had learnt to read. Another engraving between the two windows: a black bull, its head lowered, which gazed at him with a melancholy expression. This engraving had as its caption: BULL FROM THE POLDERS OF HOLSTEIN, in smaller letters than belladonna and henbane, and harder to read. But he had managed to do so after a few days, and he had even been able to copy out all these words on a pad of notepaper that Annie had given him.

"If I understand correctly, doctor, they found nothing during the course of their search?"

"I don't know. They spent several days rifling through the house from top to bottom. The other people must have hidden something there . . ."

"And no articles about this search in the newspapers at the time?"

"No."

A whimsical plan ran through Daragane's mind at that moment. With the royalties for the book of which he had only written two or three pages, he would buy the house. He would select the necessary tools: screwdrivers, hammers, crowbars, pincers, and he would devote himself to a meticulous exploration over several days. He would slowly pull out the wood panelling from the drawing room and the bedrooms and he would smash the mirrors to see what they concealed. He would set about searching for secret staircases and hidden doors. In the end he would be sure to find what he had lost, and what he had never been able to speak about to anyone.

"You probably came by bus?" Dr Voustraat asked him.

"Yes."

The doctor checked his wristwatch.

"I can't take you back to Paris by car unfortunately. The last bus for Porte d'Asnières leaves in twenty minutes."

Outside, they walked along rue de l'Ermitage. They passed in front of the long concrete building that had replaced the garden wall, but Daragane did not wish to recall this vanished wall.

"A good deal of mist," said the doctor. "It's winter already..."

Then they walked in silence, the two of them, the doctor very erect, very upright, the bearing of a former cavalry officer. Daragane could not remember having walked like this, at night, in his childhood, along the streets of Saint-Leu-la-Forêt. Except for once, at Christmas, when Annie had taken him to midnight mass.

The bus was waiting, the engine turning over. He would evidently be the only passenger.

"I've been delighted to chat with you all afternoon," said the doctor, holding out his hand. "And I'd love to hear more about your little book on Saint-Leu."

At the very moment Daragane was about to get on the bus, the doctor held him by the arm.

"I was thinking of something . . . about La Maladrerie and all those curious people we spoke about . . . The best witness could be the child who once lived there. You would need to find him . . . Don't you think so?"

"That will be very difficult, doctor."

He sat at the very rear of the bus and looked through the

window behind him. Dr Voustraat stood there motionless, probably waiting for the bus to disappear round the first corner. He gave him a wave.

IN HIS STUDY, HE DECIDED TO RECONNECT THE TELE-
phone and the answering machine in case Chantal Grippay
should try to get in touch with him. But no doubt Ottolini,
back from the casino at Charbonnières, was not letting her
out of his sight. She would have to collect the black dress
with swallows. It was hanging there, on the back of the sofa,
like those objects that don't want to leave you and follow
you around all your life. Rather like that blue Volkswagen in
his youth that he had had to get rid of after a few years.
Yet, every time he moved home, he found it parked outside
his building – and that had gone on for a long time. The car
remained faithful to him and followed him wherever he went.
But he had lost the keys. And then, one day, it had disappeared,
perhaps into one of those automobile scrap-yards, beyond
Porte d'Italie, on the site where they had begun staking out
the Autoroute du Sud.

He wished he could have found "Return to Saint-Leu-la-Forêt", the first chapter of his first book, but his search would have been pointless. That night, as he was admiring the attractive leaves in the courtyard of the building next door, he realised that he had torn up that chapter. He was certain of it.

He had also discarded a second chapter: "Place Blanche", written immediately after "Return to Saint-Leu-la-Forêt". And so he had started all over again from the beginning with the painful sense that he was correcting a false start. And yet the only memories he retained of this first novel were the two chapters he had discarded that had served as underpinning for everything else, or rather the scaffolding you remove, once the book is finished.

He had written the twenty pages of "Place Blanche" in a room at 11 rue Coustou, a former hotel. He was living in lower Montmartre again, fifteen years after discovering it because of Annie. In fact, they had ended up there, when they had left Saint-Leu-la-Forêt. And that is why he thought he could write a book more easily if he returned to the places he had known with her.

They must have changed in appearance since that time, but he was barely aware of the fact. Forty years later, in the twenty-first century, in a taxi one afternoon, he happened to be passing through the neighbourhood. The car had stopped in a traffic jam at the corner of boulevard de Clichy and rue Coustou. For a few minutes, he had not recognised anything, as though he had been struck with amnesia and was merely a stranger in his own city. But for him this was of no importance. The fronts of the buildings and the crossroads had, over the course of years, become an inner landscape that had eventually come to cover over the sleek and well-stuffed Paris of the present day. Over there, on the right, he thought he could see the garage sign in rue Coustou and he would gladly have asked the taxi driver to drop him there so that, after forty years, he could revisit his old room.

In those days, on the floor above his, they were starting the building works that would transform the old hotel bedrooms into studio flats. In order to write his book without hearing the sounds of hammering on the walls, he took shelter in a café on rue Puget that formed the corner with rue Coustou and was overlooked from his bedroom window.

In the afternoons, there were no customers in this establishment known as the Aero, a bar rather than a café, to judge by its pale wood panelling, its ornamental ceiling, its equally pale wooden frontage, with a window protected by a sort of moucharaby. A man of about forty, with dark hair, used to stand behind the bar, reading a newspaper. During the course of the afternoon, he would sometimes disappear up a small staircase. The first time, Daragane had called to him so that he could pay his bill, but to no avail. And afterwards, he grew accustomed to his absences and left him a five-franc note on the table.

He had to wait for a few days before the man spoke to him. Up until then, he ignored him deliberately. Every time Daragane ordered a coffee, the man appeared not to hear him, and Daragane was astonished when he eventually switched on the percolator. He came and placed the coffee cup on the table without even glancing at him. And Daragane sat down at the back of the room as if he himself wished to go unnoticed.

One afternoon when he had managed to correct a page of his manuscript, he heard a solemn voice:

"So, are you doing your accounts?"

He looked up. Over there, behind the bar, the man was smiling at him.

"You come at the wrong time . . . In the afternoons it's deserted here."

He walked over to his table, still with the same quizzical smile:

"May I?"

He pulled out the chair and sat down in front of him.

"What exactly are you writing?"

Daragane hesitated before replying.

"A detective story."

The other man nodded and gave him a searching stare.

"I live at the building on the corner, but there are refurbishments going on and there's too much noise to be able to work."

"The former Hôtel Puget? Opposite the garage?"

"Yes," said Daragane. "And you, have you been here long?"

He would often change the subject in order to avoid talking about himself. His method was to reply to one question with another one.

"I've always been in the neighbourhood. Before that, I ran a hotel, a little further down, on rue Laferrière . . ."

This word, Laferrière, made his heart thump. When he had left Saint-Leu-la-Forêt with Annie to come to this neighbourhood, they both lived in a room on rue Laferrière. She would be away, from time to time, and she gave him a duplicate key. "If you go for a walk, don't get lost." On a sheet of paper folded in four that he kept in his pocket, she had written: "6 rue Laferrière" in her big handwriting.

"I knew a woman who used to live there," said Daragane in an expressionless voice. "Annie Astrand."

The man looked at him in surprise.

"Then you really must have been very young. That's about twenty or so years ago."

"I'd say more like fifteen."

"I mainly knew her brother Pierre. It was he who lived in rue Laferrière. He ran the garage next door . . . but I haven't heard anything of him for a long time."

"Do you remember her?"

"Slightly . . . She was very young when she left the neighbourhood. According to what Pierre had told me, she was protected by a woman who ran a nightclub in rue de Ponthieu . . ."

Daragane wondered whether he was not confusing Annie with someone else. And yet a girlfriend of hers, Colette, often came to Saint-Leu-la-Forêt and, one day, they had driven her back to Paris by car, to a street near the Champs-Élysées gardens where the postage stamp market used to take place. Rue de Ponthieu? The two women had gone into a building together. And he had waited for Annie on the back seat of the car.

"You don't know what became of her?"

The man looked at him somewhat suspiciously.

"No. Why? Was she really a friend of yours?"

"I knew her in my childhood."

"Well, that changes everything . . . It's all in the past now . . ."

He had begun to smile again and he leant over towards Daragane.

"A longtime ago, Pierre told me that she had had some problems and that she had been in prison."

He had used the same words that Perrin de Lara had, the evening of the previous month when he had come across him sitting alone on the terrace of a café. "She had been in prison." The tone of each of the two men was different: a slightly disdainful, distant manner, in the case of Perrin de Lara, as though Daragane had obliged him to talk about someone who was not from his world; a kind of familiarity in the case of the other, since he knew "her brother Pierre" and because "being in prison" appeared to be fairly commonplace to him. Was it on account of certain customers of his who came, he had explained to Daragane, "after eleven o'clock at night"?

He thought that Annie would have given him some explanations if she was still alive. Later on, when his book had been published and he had been fortunate enough to see her again, he had not asked her a single question about this matter. She would not have replied. Neither had he mentioned the room in rue Laferrière, nor the sheet of paper folded in four on which she had written their address. He had lost that sheet of paper. And even if he had been able to keep hold of it for fifteen years and had shown it to her, she would have said: "But, Jean dear, that's not at all like my handwriting."

The man at the Aero did not know why she had been in prison. "Her brother Pierre" had not given him any details about it. But Daragane remembered that the day before they left Saint-Leu-la-Forêt she seemed nervous. She had even forgotten to come to collect him from school at half-past four, and he had returned to the house on his own. That had not really bothered him. It was easy, all you had to do was continue straight along the road. Annie was on the phone in the drawing room. She had given him a wave and had gone on talking on the phone. In the evening, she had taken him to her bedroom, and he watched her filling a suitcase with clothing. He was frightened that she might leave him alone in the house. But she had told him that tomorrow they would both be going to Paris.

In the night, he had heard voices in Annie's bedroom. He had recognised that of Roger Vincent. A little later on, the noise from the engine of the American car grew fainter and eventually subsided. He was frightened of hearing *her* car starting up. And then he fell asleep.

One late afternoon when he was leaving the Aero after having written two pages of his book – the building works in the former hotel stopped at about six o'clock in the evening – he wondered whether the walks he had been on fifteen years ago while Annie was away had taken him as far as this. There could not have been very many of these walks and they must have been shorter than he remembered. Had Annie really allowed a child to wander around alone in this neighbourhood? The address written in her handwriting on the sheet of paper folded in four – a detail that he could not have invented – was certainly proof of this.

He recalled having walked along a road at the end of which he could see the Moulin-Rouge. He had not dared go further than the central reservation of the boulevard for fear of getting lost. As a matter of fact, it would only have required a few steps for him to find himself at the spot where he was now. And the thought of this gave him a strange sensation, as though time was irrelevant. It happened fifteen years ago, he was walking on his own, very near here, in the July sunshine, and now it was December. Every time he left the Aero, it was already dark. But suddenly, for him, the seasons and the years merged together. He decided to walk as far as rue Laferrière – the same route he used to take in the past – straight on, keep straight on. The streets were on a slope and, as he walked further down, he felt certain that he was going backwards in time. The darkness would grow brighter at the bottom of rue Fontaine, it would be daylight and there would be that July sunshine. Annie had not merely written the address on the sheet of paper folded in four, but the words: SO YOU DON'T GET LOST IN THE NEIGH-BOURHOOD, in her large handwriting, an old-fashioned handwriting that was no longer taught at the school in Saint-Leu-la-Forêt.

The slope on rue Notre-Dame-de-Lorette was as steep as the previous street. You just had to let yourself glide along. A little further down. On the left. Only once had they gone back together to their room when it was dark. It was the day before they set off by train. She had her hand on his head or on his neck, a protective gesture to assure herself that he really was walking beside her. They were returning from the Hôtel Terrass beyond the bridge that overlooks the cemetery. They had gone into this hotel, and he had recognised Roger Vincent, in an armchair, at the back of the foyer. They sat down with him. Annie and Roger Vincent were talking to one another. They forgot he was there. He listened to them without understanding what they were saying. They were speaking too quietly. At one moment, Roger Vincent repeated the same thing: Annie must "take the train" and she must "leave her car in the garage". She disagreed, but she had eventually said to him: "Yes, you're right, it's more sensible." Roger Vincent had turned to him and had smiled. "Here, this is for you." And he had handed him a navy-blue folder and told him to open it. "Your passport." He had recognised himself on the photograph, one of those they had had taken in the Photo-maton booth where, on each occasion, the extreme brightness of the light had made him blink. He could read his first name and his date of birth on the opening page, but the surname was not his, it was Annie's: ASTRAND. Roger Vincent had told him in a solemn voice that he must use the same name as the "person accompanying him", and this explanation had been enough for him.

On the way back, Annie and he walked along the central reservation of the boulevard. After the Moulin-Rouge, they had taken a small street, on the left, at the end of which stood the front of a garage. They had passed through a workshop that smelt of darkness and petrol. At the very back was a glass-panelled room. A young man was standing behind a desk, the same young man who sometimes came to Saint-Leu-la-Forêt and had taken him to the Cirque Médrano one afternoon. They spoke about Annie's car, which could be seen, over there, parked alongside the wall.

He had left the garage with her, it was dark and he had wanted to read the words on the neon sign: "Grand Garage de la Place Blanche", the same words that he read again, fifteen years later, leaning out of the window of his bedroom at 11 rue Coustou. When he had switched off the light and was trying to get to sleep, reflections in the shape of trellis work were projected onto the wall, opposite his bed. He went to bed early, because of the building works that started up again at about seven o'clock in the morning. It was difficult for him to write after a bad night. In his drowsiness, he could hear Annie's voice, more and more distant, and all he could understand was the end of a sentence: ". . . SO YOU DON'T GET LOST IN THE NEIGHBOURHOOD . . ." On waking up, in this bedroom, he realised that it had taken him fifteen years to cross the street.

On that afternoon last year, 4 December 2012 – he had jotted down the date in his notebook – there was a long traffic jam and he asked the taxi driver to turn right into rue Coustou. He was mistaken when he thought he could see the garage sign from a distance, for the garage had vanished. And so too, on the same pavement, had the black wooden exterior of the Néant. On both sides, the façades of the buildings looked new, as though they were covered with a glaze or a thin layer of some colourless cellophane that had erased the cracks and stains of the past. And behind, at the very back, they must have resorted to taxidermy in order to create the empty space. On rue Puget, the woodwork and the window of the Aero had been replaced by a white wall, that kind of neutral blank whiteness that is the colour of oblivion. For over forty years, he, too, had drawn a blank over the period when he wrote that first book and over the summer when he walked on his own with the sheet of paper folded in four in his pocket: SO YOU DON'T GET LOST IN THE NEIGHBOURHOOD.

That night, on leaving the garage, Annie and he were unlikely to have changed pavements. They would certainly have walked past the Néant.

Fifteen years later, the Néant still existed. He had never felt he wanted to go inside. He was too frightened of toppling into a black hole. What is more, it seemed to him that nobody crossed its threshold. He had asked the owner of the Aero what kind of show they put on – "I believe that it's there that Pierre's sister made her debut at the age of sixteen. Apparently, the customers all sit in the darkness, with acrobats, circus riders and striptease artists who wear skull and crossbones." That night, had Annie cast a brief glance at the entrance of the establishment where she had made her "debut"?

As they crossed the boulevard, she had held his hand. For the first time, he was seeing Paris at night. They did not walk down rue Fontaine, that street he was accustomed to taking when he walked about on his own in the daytime. She led him along the central reservation. Fifteen years later, he was walking along the same central reservation, in winter, behind the fairground stalls that had been put up for Christmas and he could not take his eyes off those brightly lit neon signs that called out to him and the increasingly faint Morse code signals. It was as though they were gleaming for the last time and still belonged to the summer when he had found himself in the neighbourhood with Annie. How long had they been there? For months, for years, like those dreams that have seemed so long to you and which you realise, on waking up suddenly, have only lasted a few seconds?

As far as rue Laferrière he could feel her hand on his neck. He was still a child who might escape and get run over. At the foot of the stairs, she had put her index finger to her lips to let him know that they must go upstairs in silence.

That night, he had woken up on several occasions. He was sleeping on a couch in the same bedroom as Annie, and she was in the double bed. Their two suitcases were lying at the foot of the bed, Annie's leather case and his smaller one, made of tin. She had got up in the middle of the night and she had left the bedroom. He could hear her talking in the room next door to someone who must have been her brother, the man from the garage. He had eventually fallen asleep. Very early the following morning, she had stroked his forehead as she woke him up and they had had breakfast together, with her brother.

The three of them were sitting round a table, and she was rummaging in her handbag because she feared she might have lost the blue folder that Roger Vincent had brought to the foyer of the hotel the previous day, his "passport", in the name of "Jean Astrand". But no, it was there in her handbag. Later on, at the time of the rue Coustou room, he would ask himself when he had lost this fake passport. Probably in his early adolescence, at the time he had been sent home from his first boarding school.

Annie's brother had driven them by car to the gare de Lyon. It was difficult to walk on the pavement outside the station and in the great hall, because of the masses of people. Annie's brother was carrying the suitcases. Annie said that it was the first day of the summer holidays. She was waiting at a counter to get the train tickets, while he stayed with Annie's brother, who had put down the suitcases. You had to be careful that people did not jostle you and that the porters' trolleys did not roll over your feet. They were late, they had run to the platform, she was gripping him very hard by the wrist so that he did not get lost in the crowd, and her brother was following them with the suitcases. They had climbed onto one of the first carriages, Annie's brother behind them. Masses of people in the corridor. Her brother had put down the suitcases at the entrance to the carriage and had kissed Annie. And then, he had smiled at him and whispered in his ear: "Make sure you

remember . . . Your name is Jean Astrand now . . . Astrand."
And he barely had time to get down onto the platform and to
wave to them. The train began to pull away. There was one free
seat in one of the compartments. "You sit there," Annie had
told him. "I'll stay in the corridor." He did not want to leave her,
she had dragged him along, holding him by the shoulder. He
was frightened she might leave him there, but his seat was next
to the door of the compartment, and he could keep an eye on
her. Standing in the corridor, she did not move and, from time
to time, she turned around to smile at him. She lit a cigarette
with her silver lighter, she was pressing her forehead to the
window and she would certainly have been admiring the scen-
ery. He kept his head down in order to avoid catching the eye
of the other travellers in the compartment. He was frightened
that they might ask him questions, as adults often do when
they notice a child on his own. He would have liked to stand
up so that he could ask Annie whether their two suitcases
were still in the same place, at the entrance to the carriage, and
whether someone might steal them. She opened the door of
the compartment, leant over towards him and said to him in
a low voice: "We'll go to the restaurant car. I'll be able to sit
with you." It seemed to him as though the travellers in the
compartment were looking at both of them. And the images
follow one after the other, in fits and starts, like a worn-out

film. They are walking down the corridors of the coaches and she is holding him by the neck. He is frightened when they move from one carriage to another above the couplings where the pitching movement is so vigorous that you risk falling over. She grips his arm so that he does not lose his balance. They are sitting opposite one another, at a table in the restaurant car. Luckily, they have the table to themselves, and in any case there is hardly anyone at the other tables. It is a change from all those carriages they have just passed through where the corridors and compartments were packed. She runs her hand over his cheek and tells him that they will stay at their table as long as possible and, should no-one come to disturb them, until the end of the journey. The thing that worries him is their two suitcases, which they have left back there, at the entrance to the other carriage. He wonders whether they may lose them or whether someone may already have stolen them. He must have read a story of this kind in one of the Bibliothèque verte books that Roger Vincent had brought for him one day at Saint-Leu-la-Forêt. And it is probably on account of this that he will be haunted throughout his life by a dream: suitcases that are lost on a train, or else the train leaves with your suitcases and you are left on the platform. If he could remember all his dreams, he would now be counting hundreds and hundreds of lost suitcases.

"Don't worry, Jean dear," says Annie, smiling at him. These words reassure him. They are still sitting in the same seats after lunch. No-one else in the restaurant car. The train stops at a large station. He asks her whether they have arrived. Not yet, Annie tells him. She explains to him that it must be six o'clock in the evening and that it is always this time when you arrive in this city. Some years later, he would frequently catch the same train and he would know the name of the city where one arrives at dusk in winter. Lyon. She has taken a pack of cards from her handbag and she wants to teach him how to play patience, but he does not understand it at all.

He has never made such a long journey. No-one has come to disturb them. "They've forgotten us," Annie tells him. And the memories he still has of all this have also been worn away by forgetfulness, apart from a few more distinct images when the film slips and eventually gets stuck on one of them. Annie rummages in her bag and hands him the navy-blue folder – his passport – so that he remembers his new name carefully. In a few days' time they will cross "the frontier" to go to another country and to a city that is called "Rome". "Remember this name carefully: Rome. And I swear to you that they won't be able to find us in Rome. I've got friends there." He does not really understand what she is saying, but because she bursts out laughing, he starts to laugh as well. She plays patience again and he watches her laying the cards in rows on the table. The train stops once more at a large station, and he asks her whether they have arrived. No. She has given him the pack of cards, and he enjoys sorting them out according to their colours. Spades. Diamonds. Clubs. Hearts. She tells him that it is time to go and find the suitcases. They go back along the corridors of the coaches in the opposite direction, and she holds him sometimes by the neck, sometimes by the arm. The corridors and the compartments are empty. She says that all the passengers have got off before them. A ghost train. They find their suitcases in the same place at the entrance to the coach. It is dark and they are on the deserted platform of a very small station. They go down a lane that runs alongside the railway track. She stops in front of a door hollowed out of a surrounding wall and she takes a key from her handbag. They walk down a path in the dark. A large white house with lights on in the windows. They go into a room that is very brightly lit and has black and white tiling. In his memory, however, he confuses this house with the one in Saint-Leu-la-Forêt, probably because of the short time he spent there with Annie. The bedroom he slept in down there, for instance, seems to him to be identical to the one in Saint-Leu-la-Forêt.

Twenty years later, he happened to be on the Côte d'Azur and he had thought he recognised the little station and the lane they had walked down between the railway track and the walls of the houses. Èze-sur-Mer. He had even questioned a man with grey hair who ran a restaurant on the beach. "That must be the old Villa Embiricos on Cap Estel . . ." He had jotted down the name just in case, but when the man added, "A Monsieur Vincent had bought it during the war. Afterwards it was impounded. Now, they've turned it into a hotel", he felt afraid. No, he would not return to places for the sake of recognising them. He was too frightened that the grief, buried away until then, might unfurl through the years like a Bickford fuse.

They never go to the beach. In the afternoons, they stay in the garden, from where you can see the sea. She found a car in the garage of the house, a car that was bigger than the one at Saint-Leu-la-Forêt. In the evenings, she takes him to have dinner in the restaurant. They take the Corniche road. It is in this car, she tells him, that they will cross "the frontier" and drive as far as "Rome". On the last day, she would often leave the garden to make telephone calls and she seemed anxious. They are sitting opposite one another beneath a veranda, and he is watching her playing patience. She leans over and she frowns. She appears to be thinking a great deal before laying down one card after another, but he notices a tear trickling down her cheek, so small that you can hardly see it, as on that day, at Saint-Leu-la-Forêt, when he was sitting in the car beside her. In the night, when she speaks on the telephone in the bedroom next door, he can hear only the sound of her voice and not the words. In the morning, he is woken up by the rays of the sun that peep into his bedroom through the curtains and make orange patches on the wall. To begin with, it is almost nothing, the crunch of tyres on the gravel, the sound of an engine growing fainter, and you need a little more time to realise that there is no-one left in the house apart from you.

PATRICK MODIANO was born in Paris in 1945. His first novel, *La Place de l'étoile*, was published in 1968 when he was just twenty-two and his works have now been translated into over thirty languages around the world. He won the Austrian State Prize for European Literature in 2012, the 2010 Prix Mondial Cino Del Duca from the Institut de France for lifetime achievement, the 1978 Prix Goncourt for *Rue de boutique obscures*, and the 1972 Grand Prix du roman de l'Académie française for *Les boulevards de ceinture*. He was awarded the Nobel Prize in Literature in 2014.

EUAN CAMERON's translations include works by Julien Green, Simone de Beauvoir and Paul Morand, and biographies of Marcel Proust and Irène Némirovsky.